ENGAGED TO
THE BILLIONAIRE BOYS CLUB

CARA MILLER

Want my unreleased 5000-word story
Introducing the Billionaire Boys Club
and other free gifts from time to time?

Then join my mailing list at

http://www.caramillerbooks.com/inner-circle/

Subscribe now and read it now!

You can also follow me on Twitter and Facebook

Engaged to the Billionaire Boys Club
Copyright © 2016, Cara Miller.
All rights reserved.

"Getting even?" Kelsey asked in disbelief. "What does that mean?"

"Lisa took something away from me. I plan on returning the favor," Tyler replied as he wiped his fingers on a napkin.

"What?" Kelsey asked. She was confused.

"It doesn't matter," Tyler said. "Just trust me."

Kelsey returned to her desk with Tyler's suggestions for her contract, a green tea frappuccino, and a feeling of anxiety. Kelsey put her iPad on her desk and sat down. She turned her chair and looked out on Puget Sound as the sun set over the water. Kelsey took a sip of her icy drink, but barely tasted it.

Tyler was a mystery lately, and his conversation with Jeffrey hadn't given Kelsey any new clues. In fact, as far as Kelsey was concerned, their talk had made things even less clear.

Kelsey understood that Tyler was still upset with Lisa, but she was completely puzzled why he was refusing the opportunity to talk to her about his relationship with Kelsey. Jeffrey obviously believed that now was a good time, and as Lisa Olsen's longtime employee, Kelsey thought he might have an understanding of when to approach the fearsome CEO. On the other hand, Tyler was Lisa's son, and Kelsey had to accept that he probably knew her better than anyone. And Tyler had declared that he had nothing to say to her now.

Kelsey was trying to be patient, trying to let Tyler run his own life, even when it affected their relationship, but she was finding it difficult. She wanted to feel settled, after months of uncertainty — and right now, Tyler Olsen wasn't helping.

Jeffrey's visit seemed to have no effect on Tyler's actions over the next day. As always, he worked nonstop, as did Kelsey and the rest of the office. There was so much to do, and not enough time to do it.

Over the past few months, Kelsey had begun to accept that this would always be true when she worked for Bill Simon, so when the opportunity to get out of the office arrived, she shouldn't postpone it for work. The work would always be there. So when a surprise invitation arrived, Kelsey didn't hesitate. She said yes.

"Are you allowed to be here?" Kelsey teased as she slid into the booth at the Dahlia Lounge.

"If we get caught, we were discussing Samson," Alex Carsten replied with a grin.

Kelsey looked at the decor. "This is much nicer than our last venue," she said.

Alex laughed. "I felt like I needed to make that up to you," he replied.

"You don't."

"How are you, Miss North?"

"Good."

"How's Simon?"

"Fine."

"Keeping you busy?"

"Very."

"No surprise there. Should we order?"

"We should," Kelsey replied with a smile.

After perusing the menu and ordering, Alex leaned back in his seat.

"So what's next for Miss North?"

"What do you mean?" Kelsey asked.

"You've been at Simon for almost four months. Surely you're planning on leaving."

Kelsey shook her head. "Actually, I'm not. I'm going to stay for a while."

"Seriously, Kelsey? Do I need to stage an intervention?"

"I like it. It took me a while to get used to working all of the time, but Bill's got really interesting work, and I have a lot of responsibility."

"So I hear. Going up against Mary your first year," Alex said.

"I suppose," Kelsey said.

"Mary said she was surprised. She expected you to be quiet during the meeting. Clearly she wasn't paying attention while you were with us."

"Samson's my case," Kelsey shrugged. "So are they going to settle?"

"I think Mary's working on them," Alex said confidentially.

The waiter delivered their drinks, then left. Alex took a sip of his. "I understand that Mr. Tyler Olsen also works for Bill Simon."

"He does," Kelsey said.

"And you're still alive?" Alex asked.

"Lisa Olsen couldn't care less, as far as I can tell," Kelsey replied.

"Really? Are you still going out with him?" Alex asked.

"No," Kelsey replied.

"Is that weird?"

"Not really," Kelsey lied. She trusted Alex, but she wasn't interested in discussing her complicated relationship with Tyler.

"You're all about business, aren't you, Miss North? You were at Collins Nicol too."

"I've wanted to be a lawyer for a long time," Kelsey said.

"And now you are one. Congratulations on passing the bar."

"You saw my name on the list?" Kelsey asked.

"Of course. I'm your mentor," Alex said, giving her a wink.

Kelsey and Alex sat in the restaurant for hours, enjoying dinner and just talking about their respective jobs. Alex dished the gossip from Collins Nicol, including Jamie Harding's reprimand for sexual harassment of one of the secretaries, and the expansion of the Trusts and Estates group. He laughed at Kelsey's tales of late night filings.

"I'll drive you home," Alex said, as he helped Kelsey with her coat at the door. "Where do you live now?"

"Downtown," Kelsey replied.

"Where?"

"Harbor Steps," Kelsey said, pulling her hair out from under the collar of the coat.

"Seriously?"

"It's close to work," Kelsey hedged. "And it's not like I spend money on anything else."

"Maybe Bill Simon pays better than I thought," Alex said as they walked outside.

Kelsey laughed.

"I'm glad to see that you're doing well," Alex said thoughtfully.

"Me, too."

"I was a little worried about you."

"Were you?"

"Just a little. Not everyone survives a fight with Lisa Olsen."

"I'm pretty tough," Kelsey said.

"Yeah, I see that. You're like a cat. Do you always land on your feet?"

Kelsey thought back to her troubled youth, and to the dramas of the last year.

"Yes," she said, with confidence.

On Thursday evening Zach arrived as usual, and Kelsey met him at the door. He was holding a large bag, and Kelsey couldn't help but take a nervous breath. She glanced at the bag, then at Zach's dark eyes.

"It's dinner, Miss North," Zach said with a grin.

Kelsey breathed out in relief as Zach walked into the office, and she closed the door behind him.

"I think Mr. Olsen has enough money for now," Zach continued, as they walked to the conference room table outside Kelsey's office.

Kelsey giggled. She knew that Zach was alluding to the hundred thousand dollars of Tyler's that was sitting in her safe deposit box, but she couldn't help but joke, "I think Mr. Olsen will always have enough money."

"Yeah, that's probably true," Zach said, laughing.

"So what did you bring me?" Kelsey asked as they sat down.

"Italian. From that place you and Jess went to," Zach said.

"Thanks," Kelsey said. The food at Scucci had been amazing.

"You're welcome. You know it's still Ms. Olsen's favorite."

"I've heard," Kelsey replied. Lisa Olsen was still major news right now. Between her new relationship and Tactec's falling stock price, both the tabloids and the business sections had plenty to write about.

"So," Zach continued, "I figured you wouldn't be going back any time soon."

"No, I don't think so," Kelsey agreed as Zach began removing take-out containers from the bag. "So are things with the merger as bad as everyone is reporting?" Kelsey had read an article this morning about a second sick-out at Koh Software, Tactec's newest California acquisition.

"Worse," Zach replied. "Lisa needs to go back to California, but her latest boy-toy thinks she works too much."

Kelsey glanced at Zach, who was breaking a piece of garlic bread. He shrugged and gave her a smile.

"My mother was in a talkative mood last weekend," he commented Kelsey nodded in understanding. Zach's mother, Keiko Payne, was Lisa Olsen's closest friend. Of course she would know what was happening in Lisa Olsen's life. Kelsey thoughtfully twirled a bit of pasta on her fork.

"So what does Lisa think about Tyler?" Kelsey asked.

Zach smiled. "It's interesting you ask that," he said. From the look on his face, Zach knew that Tyler had turned down Lisa Olsen's dinner invitation. "Well, despite the fact that Lisa is completely confident in her decision to meddle in Tyler's personal relationships, she is concerned about the fact that she hasn't seen her son for almost six months, even though he lives less than thirty minutes away."

"Doesn't she work across the street one day a week? Why doesn't she just go to Simon's office?" But as the words came out of Kelsey's mouth, she knew the answer. So did Zach.

"Simon's not going to let Lisa Olsen come into his office. They hate each other," Zach said confidently.

Kelsey nodded and bit into her garlic bread. Everyone said that about Bill Simon and Lisa Olsen, but she had never seen any evidence of their animosity. Then again, Simon's firm had no current lawsuits against Tactec. Maybe if the firm took on one of those cases, Kelsey would see their dispute up close.

"Anyway, Lisa's kind of upset. My mother told her that Tyler would come around."

"But you know better?" Kelsey asked.

"As do you," Zach said. "Tyler's not going to see Lisa any time soon."

"That must be weird," Kelsey mused.

"What?" Zach asked.

"Not talking to your parents."

"Yeah," Zach agreed. Kelsey knew that in addition to working with his parents, Zach was also close to them. "Does that bother you?"

"A little," Kelsey admitted. "But they're Tyler's parents, not mine. He has to decide what kind of relationship that he wants with them."

"Would your parents forbid you to date someone?" Zach asked.

"No," Kelsey admitted.

"The problem with Lisa, is that she still has the power to enforce her rules. If Tyler hadn't agreed to stop dating you, Lisa would have continued to attack you until you were begging to break up with him."

"I know," Kelsey said. "I don't blame Tyler. I don't even blame Lisa."

"Do you blame yourself?" Zach asked, and Kelsey looked at him, startled. Zach's eyes met hers, and after a moment of thought, Kelsey nodded.

"I do," Kelsey admitted.

"You shouldn't. You're good for Tyler, and it doesn't matter what happened in your past," Zach replied.

"I know it shouldn't," Kelsey said. "But I can't help but think that Lisa wouldn't have reacted the way that she did if Tyler had been dating someone else."

In fact, Kelsey was sure of it. Lisa Olsen had married an artist, and from her relatively brief dealings with her, Kelsey thought that she was pretty down-to-earth. Lisa had focused on Kelsey's criminal past, not her modest upbringings, when she had spoken to Kelsey.

"Tyler doesn't want anyone else. Tyler wants you," Zach pointed out.

"Maybe Tyler needs to change his mind," Kelsey said.

"I think that the odds of that are zero."

Kelsey sighed. She thought so too.

On Friday, Kelsey went back home to change after her run at the gym. Once she was wearing her new blue wool dress, she walked over to the offices of Lewis and Lindsay, where her CLE was being held. Once she was registered, she settled into a day of lectures about IP licensing.

At 5 p.m., Kelsey was putting her iPad into her tote bag, when Brandon Kinnon walked over to her.

"Hi, Brandon," she said, looking up at him.

"Hey, Kels," Brandon said. "Tyler told me you would be here. Can you give this to him?" he asked, holding out a memory stick.

"OK," Kelsey said, taking it and putting it into the side pocket of her tote.

"How are things?" Brandon asked.

"Fine," Kelsey said, standing and slinging her tote over her arm. "You?"

"Busy," Brandon replied. Kelsey smiled. She knew without knowing that Brandon's busyness was because of Tyler, not because of his work for Lewis and Lindsay.

"I'll tell Tyler you said 'Hi'," Kelsey said to him.

"Tell Tyler to stop sending me things to do," Brandon said with a grin. "Have a good night, Kels."

"Bye, Brandon," Kelsey replied.

Kelsey reached the office for the first time all day at 5:15 p.m., and to her surprise, it was in a state of panic. Marie explained as Millie took a call at the front desk.

"Just as we were about to finalize the Adamson deal, opposing counsel sent over a list of undisclosed contingent liabilities."

Kelsey understood the problem instantly. When two companies were about to merge, or one of them was buying the other, the lesser company was required to tell the acquiring company if there were any liabilities that were outstanding, like debt or lawsuits. This information allowed the acquiring company to determine what they were willing to pay for the company, or whether they wanted to go through with the deal at all. A new list of contingent liabilities meant that all of the previous calculations of the company's worth were now useless.

"Adamson's CEO announced to the press that he isn't sure if the deal is worth it with these new liabilities, and the phone's been ringing off the hook," Marie said, as Rina, the M&A paralegal, ran past the front desk, heading towards Bill's side of the office.

"What can I do to help?" Kelsey asked. The work that she had on her own desk could wait until later.

"Let Bill know you're back. He'll tell you what to do," Marie said.

Kelsey walked over to Bill's office, where Rina was talking, and she waved her hand at Bill. He saw her through the window and nodded. Kelsey walked past the front desk, and back to her office. She sat, put on her slippers and began working on her own cases. Bill walked into her office twenty minutes later.

"How was the CLE?" he asked.

"Really great," Kelsey replied.

"You can give the team a report later," Bill said. "You heard about Adamson?"

"Yes," Kelsey replied.

"Tyler and Tori are working through the new calculations. But Tyler was working on a brief for the Simmons case, which needs to be filed tonight. Do you think you can finish it?"

"Sure," Kelsey said.

"Ask me if you need help," Bill said. Kelsey looked back down at her computer, located Tyler's unfinished brief in their shared documents, and got to work.

Tyler walked into Kelsey's office at 7:30. She hadn't left her desk once since she had arrived.

"Hi, Kelsey," Tyler said, sitting in one of her client chairs.

"Hey," Kelsey replied, looking up at him.

"Thanks for doing my work," Tyler said.

"It's not a problem," Kelsey replied.

"Have you eaten?" Tyler asked.

"Not without you," Kelsey replied, and Tyler smiled.

"I'll order. How is it going?"

"OK. I should be done by nine," Kelsey replied.

"With or without a dinner break?" Tyler asked.

"With," Kelsey said. "You had done the most difficult arguments. Oh, here," she added. She reached into her tote and took out the memory stick. She handed it to Tyler, who placed it into his pants pocket.

"Thanks," Tyler said. He stretched his arms. "I see you're wearing my favorite dress," he commented.

"Is this your favorite?" Kelsey asked, as she typed.

"You know it is," Tyler replied huskily.

Kelsey glanced at him. "Stop being a pain," she warned.

"Are you saying that I can't lust after you?" Tyler asked.

"That's exactly what I'm saying," Kelsey replied.

"How about after I marry you?" Tyler asked.

"I told you to stop being a pain," Kelsey warned.

Tyler laughed and stood up. "I'll order," he said, and walked out of the room.

On Saturday, Ryan and Jessica invited Kelsey to Bob's house for dinner. Tyler and the M&A team were still at work, but Kelsey and Jake weren't needed, so they had both left. As Jessica pulled up to the house in Medina, Kelsey was surprised to see that a gigantic gate was now blocking their access to the three houses Bob and Lisa owned. The gate swung open as Jessica's car approached, and they drove straight through without stopping at the guard house which was just outside the gate.

"When did this happen?" Kelsey asked, looking behind the car as Jessica drove through the gate and turned toward Bob's house.

"A few weeks ago," Jessica said.

"Why?" Kelsey asked.

"With Lisa's purchase of the house next to her, there was enough space to build the gate without crowding the houses," Ryan said from the passenger seat.

"I see," Kelsey said, as Jessica parked.

They piled out of the car and walked into the house, each carrying a bag of the groceries that Ryan had bought on the way. Kelsey glanced over to Lisa Olsen's main house. She knew from the media that Ms. Olsen was back in California, once again trying to salvage her acquisition. As for Bob, he was in New York on Tactec business.

After putting the groceries away, the trio changed and headed to the indoor swimming pool. As far as Kelsey could tell, Bob's house was empty, save for the butler who had greeted them at the door.

Jessica floated on her back in the pool as Kelsey lay on one of the comfortable lounge chairs which surrounded it. The fading sun shone through the glass that surrounded the pool, and Kelsey enjoyed the gentle warmth. Ryan sat next to her on a lounge, flipping through a cookbook.

"How's work?" Kelsey asked.

"Boring," Ryan replied.

"What do you have to do?" Kelsey asked.

"Nothing," Ryan replied.

Kelsey glanced at him. When he had joined Tactec in the summers, Ryan had been expected to work on legal projects. "Why?" she asked.

Ryan shrugged. "Lisa's too busy to care," he replied. "And if she doesn't tell Sydney to assign me something, Sydney won't."

"So what are you doing?" Kelsey asked.

"Research," Ryan replied.

"For what?" Kelsey asked. Ryan glanced at her, and Kelsey realized that like her, Ryan was bound by confidentiality rules. "Sorry," she said.

"It's OK," Ryan replied. "It's not for Tactec," he commented.

Now it was Kelsey's turn to look at Ryan. "Then who is it for?" she asked.

"Tyler," Ryan replied unconcernedly.

"You're working on Tyler's project at work?" Kelsey asked.

"I don't have anything else to do," Ryan replied. "It's that, or come up with new recipes. I have to be in the office."

"Maybe you should talk to Bob," Kelsey commented. "There's no reason for you to go in if you don't have anything to do."

"I did talk to him, but he said it's good for me. He did say that if Jess gets pregnant, we can take some time off. Speaking of," Ryan began, "why do you think Jess isn't pregnant yet?"

Kelsey blushed a little at her next words, but she needed to give Ryan some context. "Even if you're trying, it sometimes takes a few months."

"Why?" Ryan asked.

"Timing. There's only a short window when someone can get pregnant," Kelsey said.

"How long?"

"About six days a month," Kelsey said confidently. She wasn't a biology major for nothing.

"Oh," Ryan said in disappointment. "Jess told me to be patient. Now I understand why. Do you know which days in the month?"

"Jess can calculate them," Kelsey said.

"Really?" Ryan asked curiously.

"Sure."

"Jess?" Ryan called.

"Yes?" Jessica called back from the pool.

"Do you know how to calculate the days when you can get pregnant?" Ryan asked.

"Are you bothering Kelsey?" Jessica asked. She flipped off her back and swam to the side of the pool.

"Yes. Do you know?" Ryan replied.

"Yes, Ryan. I know," Jessica said with amusement. "It's called Natural Family Planning."

"Can you teach me?" Ryan asked.

"Sure, but why?" Jessica said.

"Because you're not allowed to leave the bed on those six days," Ryan said seriously. Kelsey laughed, and Jessica splashed some water toward Ryan.

"You're crazy," Jessica said.

"I want babies," Ryan pouted.

"Just wait. Don't be so impatient. They'll show up when they're ready," Jessica said from the pool.

"Suppose they aren't ready for a few years?" Ryan asked.

"Then you'll wait," Jessica replied.

Ryan sighed.

"Ryan, most couples can get pregnant within a year," Kelsey said.

"Suppose we aren't most?" Ryan said.

"Then we'll go to the doctor and find out what's wrong," Jessica said unconcernedly.

"Why doesn't this bother you?" Ryan asked unhappily.

"Because I like being married to you, and I don't need kids right away to be happy," Jessica replied.

Ryan smiled at her. "You like being married to me?" he asked delightedly.

"I do," Jessica said. "Even though you're crazy."

"Crazy for you," Ryan said happily.

On Sunday, Kelsey was reading her Kindle when her phone rang.

"Hi, Dylan," she said, answering it.

"Hey, Kels," Dylan replied. "It's been a while. How are you?"

"I'm good," Kelsey replied, sitting up. "What's going on?"

"I just wanted to talk to you. I'm not sure we ended our last call on such a good note," Dylan commented. Kelsey agreed. Dylan wasn't happy about the fact that Tyler was still in her life, and had said so.

"I guess," Kelsey said.

"Are you OK? Maybe I should have asked you that before," Dylan said.

"I'm fine, Dylan," Kelsey said.

"And your parents?"

"They're fine too. Haven't you talked to my mom lately?" Kelsey asked.

"Not for a while. I've been busy with school," Dylan replied.

"How is school?" Kelsey asked. Dylan was now in his second year of law school in Portland.

"It's fine."

"So what are you specializing in?" Kelsey asked.

"Environmental law," Dylan said.

"And how does your family feel about that?" Kelsey asked. The Shaws owned a large restaurant chain, and with two sons, she knew that they were hoping that at least one of their children would be involved in the business.

"They aren't happy," Dylan admitted. "But they'll deal."

"How's Ian?"

"Well, you'll be happy to know that he switched from chemistry to biology."

"Really, that's great," Kelsey said. Ian went to Portland State, just as Kelsey and Dylan had. "But why?"

"He was being crushed by one of his organic chemistry classes, and he decided that he'd rather stay in school an extra year than not graduate at all," Dylan replied.

"I doubt it was that bad," Kelsey said. Dylan didn't think much of his younger brother.

"It was worse. I'm sugarcoating it for you," Dylan replied.

Kelsey laughed. "You should work on getting along with Ian," she commented.

"Please," Dylan said dismissively. "So when are you coming to Portland?"

"Dylan, I'm lucky to see my apartment. I'm not coming to Portland any time soon," Kelsey replied.

"That's too bad. There are lots of new restaurants here."

"You'll have to tell me about them," Kelsey replied.

There was a pause, then Dylan said, "I miss seeing you Kels."

"Me, too. You could come up. I have Sundays free."

"Maybe."

"Do you have a new girlfriend?"

"Yup," Dylan replied.

"And?"

"She's not the one either," Dylan replied.

"You'll find her."

"One day. There's no hurry," Dylan agreed. "I'm afraid to ask, but how's Olsen?"

"Fine."

"OK, that's enough." Dylan said, and Kelsey laughed. Kelsey could hear Dylan laugh too. He paused, then said,

"You should move back to Portland, then we could hang out together again."

"I like Seattle."

"There isn't a big difference between the two," Dylan pointed out.

"I know, but I'm closer to home here," Kelsey replied.

"Barely," Dylan said. "Anyway, you don't go home much."

"It's nice to know that it isn't far," Kelsey replied. "And I always wanted to live in Seattle."

"Yeah, but with your job, you don't have time to do anything."

"Well, that is true," Kelsey agreed. "It's OK, I like it anyway."

"Fine. You can stay for a while, but I do expect you to come visit me. Next year."

"Oh, do you?"

"Yes. You'll come down and we'll spend the weekend together, like we're in college again," Dylan said firmly.

"Can I see Ian too?" Kelsey asked in amusement.

"No," Dylan replied, and Kelsey laughed again. There was another pause, then Dylan said, "Miss you, Kels. I'll talk to you soon."

"OK, Dylan. Bye."

"Bye, Kelsey," Dylan said, and they disconnected.

Kelsey barely saw Tyler at work the next day. The entire M&A team at Simon and Associates was frantically working to get their deal back on track. Bill Simon was swamped and unable to assign projects, so Jake and Kelsey both had time to catch up on their work. Kelsey was grateful for the opportunity to get some things done, because next week her parents would come to Seattle to see her get sworn into the bar.

Tuesday, Kelsey looked out of her front office window, and out onto the large conference table that was positioned directly outside. Ingrid was directing Millie in the organization of a number of documents which lay on the table, and Kelsey watched them thoughtfully.

Ingrid, as always, was dressed professionally, and today she was wearing an ice-blue dress, her blonde hair neatly French-braided. Every time Kelsey saw her, she had the thought that a Scandinavian princess could probably take tips from Ingrid. The way she carried herself, her seemingly effortless elegance — Ingrid was a classic beauty.

And of course, she had to be Tyler's secretary.

Kelsey refused to admit to herself that she was jealous, although she knew that she was, and she knew that she had no reason to be. Although Tyler was still especially pleasant to his secretary, Kelsey also knew that he wasn't in love with her. It still grated on her when she saw them together, as she had earlier today, when Tyler had dropped by the table to ask about a document.

It wasn't Ingrid that Kelsey was upset about. It was what she represented.

Perfection.

Kelsey hated seeing Ingrid, because deep in Kelsey's heart, she believed that Ingrid was the type of girl that Tyler should be with. Smart, professional, beautiful, and as far as Kelsey could see, flawless. The kind of person that Lisa Olsen would have no issues with.

Sometimes Kelsey felt bad that Tyler had chosen her. One day, he would be CEO of his family's empire, and he would need someone by his side to support him, to smile at the press, to give tours of his palatial estate, and eventually to give him an heir. Lisa Olsen knew this, which was why she had objected to Kelsey. She believed that Kelsey wasn't suited to this role. And despite her love for Tyler, Kelsey wasn't sure that she was suited to it either.

What would it mean to be married to a billionaire? Kelsey had thought about what it would mean to be married to Tyler, of course. She imagined busy weekdays, relaxed weekends, and lots of love. But Tyler wasn't just another guy. She knew it, and so did he, but both of them had ignored it until it was too late, and Lisa Olsen had stepped in.

But nothing had changed. They were still pretending that they could make it work. That the fact that Tyler had an image to maintain — and two billion dollars to manage — wouldn't get in the way of their relationship. However, whenever Kelsey saw Ingrid, and saw Tyler next to her, she couldn't stop asking if she was kidding herself. Perhaps it was time to step aside and let Lisa Olsen pick someone like Ingrid to be Tyler's bride.

Rationally, Kelsey believed this. That one day, she could sit with Tyler, and tell him to find someone else. Someone like Ingrid who could be a billionaire's wife, and do and be all of the things that needed to be done.

But as Kelsey looked out of the window, and Tyler stepped back into her frame of vision with another question for Ingrid, Kelsey knew that it would never happen. She would never be able to let him go.

On Wednesday, the M&A team finally seemed to come up for air. The new calculations had been made, the CEO of the acquiring company had been appeased, and the respective boards were reviewing a revised purchase cost. Tyler and Tori had headed over to the client's offices to work, but before they left Tyler had managed to stop long enough to have a quick lunch with Kelsey.

Zach arrived at Kelsey's office in high spirits on Thursday evening.

"It's quiet," he noted, as he watched Kelsey lock the front door behind him.

"They're still working on the acquisition," Kelsey commented.

"Right, Tyler said it had exploded," Zach said as they walked back to Kelsey's office.

"It's coming back together," Kelsey replied.

"Deals fall apart sometimes," Zach shrugged as he sat in one of the client chairs. "What are we eating tonight?"

"Whatever," Kelsey replied.

"Are you OK?" Zach asked in concern.

"Tired," Kelsey replied.

"That's not it. Miss North has boundless energy," Zach replied knowingly.

Kelsey sighed.

"You can tell me," Zach cooed.

Kelsey looked at Zach, and he grinned.

"Spill," he said directly.

"Has Tyler thought about being married to someone like me would mean for him?" Kelsey blurted out. She had been thinking about it ever since she had watched Ingrid, and it was still troubling her.

Zachary looked at her curiously. "What do you mean?"

"Zach, don't be naive," Kelsey said irritably. "Tyler's a billionaire."

"So?"

"So, he's going to be expected to have a glamorous wife. Arm candy."

"And?" Zach said, and Kelsey glared at him.

"I'm not arm candy," Kelsey said, and Zach laughed.

"No, I suppose that's true. You're a bit too smart to be considered that. But I'm still not sure what you mean."

Kelsey sighed. She was surprised to have to explain this to Zach but she pressed on.

"Zach, billionaires always seem to have these wives that are magazine-ready. It seems to be part of the role."

"I think you're thinking about millionaires' wives," Zach replied.

"What do you mean?"

"Kelsey, billionaires marry whoever they want. They aren't worried about money or their social standing. They have a billion dollars. Who's going to judge them?"

Kelsey thought about Zach's words for a moment. She supposed that he had a point. It wasn't like she had done a study of the women who were married to billionaires.

"The people you see in magazines aren't reality. They're trying to present an image so they can prove to other people that they're really rich, so they can be invited to the best parties and make better business deals.

Tyler's never, ever going to have that problem."

Zach read the look in Kelsey's eyes and added, "That's why Lisa's not going to win this one. She shouldn't even care who Tyler marries. She's just upset that she didn't know about you."

Kelsey didn't believe that was the only reason, but she was silent so Zach could press on.

"Let Tyler worry about whether you're good enough for him. Because you are." He smiled at her.

"Thanks, Zach."

"You're welcome. Let's order dinner."

On Saturday afternoon, Kelsey sat in the mall, sipping a mocha and waiting for Jessica, who had messaged Kelsey to let her know that she was running late. Jessica and Ryan had gone to Lisa Olsen's house for a morning yoga lesson, and it had run overtime. Ryan was staying at Lisa's to have a cooking lesson with Margaret.

"Sorry, sorry," Jessica said thirty minutes later, sitting across from Kelsey.

"It's fine," Kelsey replied as Jessica put her large designer bag onto the table.

"What are you drinking?" Jessica asked.

"Mocha," Kelsey replied.

"I'm going to get something. Any requests?"

"No, thanks," Kelsey replied. Jessica pulled her hot pink wallet out of her bag and walked over to the counter. A few moments later, she sat back down, an icy granita in her hand.

"What a morning," Jess sighed, tossing the wallet back into the bag and taking a long sip of her drink.

"What happened?" Kelsey asked.

Jessica shook her head in annoyance.

"We were about fifteen minutes into class, which was great by the way, and someone walks into the room and tells Lisa that she has a phone call. She tells the teacher to pause the class while she takes it. Five minutes later, the same assistant comes in and tells Sydney that Lisa wants her."

"Sydney was there?" Kelsey asked. Sydney Klein was the Chief Legal Officer of Tactec, and from Kelsey's understanding, a friend of Lisa Olsen.

"Sydney, Zach's mom, and half of the Tactec executive committee," Jessica said, taking another sip of her drink. Her large engagement ring flashed in the bright lights of the mall. "So there goes Sydney. Twenty minutes later, the rest of us are sitting around with our dried sweat, and Lisa and Sydney walk in all excited. It turns out that Lisa had hired a new CFO."

"Another one?" Kelsey asked.

"This one's a woman," Jessica said. "Everyone hopes that Lisa takes a little more time before she fires her."

Kelsey understood. There was a very long line of fired Tactec Chief Financial Officers.

"After they get settled back on their mats, Lisa requests that the teacher start again. Like he's going to say no. Anyway, that's why I'm late."

"It's fine, Jess. I don't have anything to do for the rest of the day. I'm glad you were able to make it."

"I wouldn't miss an opportunity to hang out with you, Kels. You're always so busy."

"True," Kelsey agreed. "How's work for you?"

"I work about ten minutes a day," Jessica said. "On the other hand, I've been doing a lot of reading."

"Why don't you have anything to do?"

"Honestly, I think that Bob's just trying to get Ryan and me out of the house," Jessica replied.

"You could work somewhere else," Kelsey said.

"I know, but since I'm trying to get pregnant, I don't really want the stress. Maybe I'll look later. It's OK for now."

"Is Ryan still driving you crazy?" Kelsey asked.

"Completely," Jessica said. But there was a smile on her face. "So what are we buying today?"

"Nothing," Kelsey replied.

Jessica frowned. "I didn't invite you out to buy nothing," she said.

"I don't need anything."

"You never need anything," Jessica replied. "It doesn't matter." Jessica swung her hair and let her curls brush her neck. "We're buying things anyway."

After they finished their drinks, Jessica led Kelsey out of the mall and down the street to a designer boutique. Two thousand dollars later, after an hour-long stop at a second clothing store, the girls returned to the exclusive department store which anchored the mall.

Jessica opened the door with a flourish, her new purchases swinging on her arms. Kelsey followed her in amusement. Although Kelsey wasn't a big shopper, Jessica seemed to really enjoy it, and it was nice to spend time with her.

Their first stop was the cosmetic area, which featured companies that Kelsey had not heard of. Jess pulled Kelsey over to the counter of a French makeup company, and before Kelsey knew what was going on, the woman behind the counter was demonstrating the smokey eye look on Kelsey's eyelids.

"You look hot," Jess said as they headed up the stairs. Kelsey frowned. Although she had to admit that her eyes looked pretty, it wasn't exactly the look she normally wore on a Sunday afternoon. Frankly, there was a part of Kelsey that really wanted a makeup-remover-soaked tissue so she could look normal again. She suppressed the feeling and followed Jess upstairs.

Twenty minutes later, Jess was looking at her heel-clad foot, while Kelsey stood next to a full-length mirror, standing in heels of her own.

"Those look great," Jessica said to her.

"They do. But I don't have anywhere to wear them," Kelsey commented.

"Wear them to dinner with us sometime," Jessica said.

"You guys don't care if I wear sneakers," Kelsey replied.

Jessica grinned. "True, but you should get those anyway."

Kelsey turned back to the mirror. The shoes were fabulous. Kelsey sighed. At least she didn't have a rent payment to worry about.

The girls arrived at Jessica's condo for dinner. Ryan was in the kitchen when they walked in, arms full of shopping bags, one of which included Kelsey's new shoes. They placed the bags on the floor next to the door.

"Hi, Jess!" Ryan said happily. "Hi, Kels."

"Hey, Ryan," Kelsey said as Jessica walked into the kitchen.

"So how was the rest of your afternoon?" Jessica asked, giving Ryan a kiss.

"Weird," Ryan replied, wiping his hands on a towel and giving Jess a hug.

"Why?" Jess asked, leaning against the counter and picking up a piece of carrot.

Ryan brushed Jess' curls gently with his hand. "After everyone left, things felt really tense."

"What do you mean?"

"Well," Ryan said, thinking, "when Margaret was helping me, she asked me about Tyler. Was he eating, was he OK working in the same office with Kelsey, stuff like that."

"She's worried," Kelsey said, a little sadly. She knew how close Tyler and Margaret were.

"She said that he hadn't called her in months, and although Jeffrey said that he was fine, Margaret didn't believe Jeffrey because Jeffrey was insisting that Tyler was fine up until the moment that Tyler disappeared from Darrow."

"You told her Tyler was OK?" Kelsey asked.

"Yeah, but I'm not sure she believes me either," Ryan said. "Margaret said that she had been looking forward to seeing Tyler when Lisa invited him to dinner, and that everyone in the house was shocked when Tyler said no."

Jessica listened, but said nothing. Kelsey wondered what she was thinking of this conversation, but she wasn't going to ask.

"Then when Lisa walked into the kitchen, Margaret stopped talking about Tyler in mid-sentence. Lisa sat at the kitchen table, Margaret poured her a glass of the smoothie that had been sitting in the blender, but when Lisa thanked her, Margaret completely ignored her and went back to the pantry."

Jess took another carrot, and ate it.

"Lisa finished her drink, and asked me to come talk to her in the living room," Ryan continued. "She asked me basically the same questions that Margaret had asked me. Was Tyler eating? Was he OK? She didn't ask about you, Kelsey. Margaret had, though."

Kelsey nodded.

"Lisa wanted to know when I had last seen Tyler, and she asked whether he was working a lot. That was pretty much it."

"Interesting," Jess said blandly, and she left the room. Ryan's blue eyes followed her, then he turned to Kelsey.

"Thank you for telling me, Ryan," Kelsey said.

"I wish Jess would forgive him," Ryan commented.

"She'll come around," Kelsey said comfortingly.

"Did Tyler say why he said no?" Ryan asked.

"Not really," Kelsey hedged.

"He hasn't been in that house for months, but it still revolves around him," Ryan commented.

"What do you mean?" Kelsey said puzzled.

"Tyler always says that Lisa is obsessed with work and doesn't care about his feelings, but she's really worried about him. Everyone in the house is. I wish he'd go talk to Lisa."

"He's not going to," Kelsey commented. "Not any time soon."

"He has no idea how much he's upsetting her," Ryan said.

"Actually," Kelsey commented. "I think he does."

On Sunday, Kelsey went on a long run along the waterfront. Per usual, it was drizzling, but Kelsey barely noticed the weather. This was her time to think, and as always she had a lot to think about.

Tyler, as always, was at the top of her list. He seemed healthy once again, and he was always happy to see her. Kelsey was concerned that he was working too much, but she knew that would never change for him. He would eventually be Tactec's CEO, after all.

Or would he? Tyler had said that he wouldn't join Tactec without being with her again, and Kelsey knew Tyler well enough to know that he meant what he had said. Over the past few months of working together, their relationship had transformed from the shock of being back in the same place together, to friendship without kissing, and back to what Kelsey knew was love.

Kelsey knew that Tyler had never stopped loving her, and she him, but thanks to Lisa Olsen, both of them had been afraid to express it. Time had softened Kelsey's fear, and whatever Tyler was working on seemed to be lessening his concerns that Lisa would go after Kelsey again. So now, private moments with Tyler were filled with gentle flirting and quiet declarations of love. Kelsey missed his touch though, and she knew that he missed hers, because he had told her so. But for now, that barrier remained.

Kelsey rushed around her office late on Tuesday afternoon. Her parents were waiting at Starbucks, so they could all go to the King County Courthouse together. Jake appeared at her doorway.

"Kels, are you ready?"

"One second," Kelsey said. She reached into her top desktop drawer and pulled out her wallet and a Chanel lipstick. It had been her favorite since Jess had brought it back from Paris, and Kelsey loved the scent of roses whenever she opened it.

"Let's go," she said excitedly.

She and Jake took the elevator downstairs. Tyler and Tori were already on the courthouse side of downtown, having been working at their M&A client's office for most of the day. Kelsey stepped confidently across the tiled floors of the building in her Christian Louboutin kitten heels. She was wearing the black wrap St. John dress that Tyler had bought for her in law school, her new pearls were around her neck, and her platinum-blonde hair rested in a low ponytail on her shoulder.

"Kelsey!" her mother said as she walked into Starbucks. Kelsey walked over to her mother and gave her a hug.

"What happened to Kelsey?" her father said, as he was hugging her.

"What do you mean?"

"No skinned knees? No ripped jeans?" her father teased.

"Funny, Dad," Kelsey said. "Mom, Dad, this is Jake. He's the other IP lawyer in my firm."

"Hi," Jake said, shaking both of their hands.

"Are you being sworn in today too?" Mrs. North said, picking up her drink from the table.

"I am," Jake said with pleasure.

"Congratulations," Mr. North said to him.

"Jake's family couldn't come today," Kelsey said.

"My wife has the sniffles," Jake added.

"We'll cheer for you," Mr. North said.

"No cheering," Kelsey said. "This is serious."

"Can I take pictures?" her father asked.

"Of course," Kelsey said, as she and Jake led them out of Starbucks, and out of the building.

"Good. Otherwise your grandmother would have my head," Mr. North commented.

"I'm sorry Grandma couldn't come," Kelsey said.

"She is too, but she had waited two months for an appointment with her doctor, and she didn't think she should miss it. She said she'll come for a long visit at Christmas."

"Yay," Kelly North said under her breath. Kelsey glared at her as they crossed the street.

"So Jake, do you work so many hours that you can't call your parents?" Dan North said, teasing Kelsey.

"I work so many hours, I don't remember what my son looks like," Jake replied.

"You have a son?" Mrs. North asked, as the light changed and they crossed Seneca Street.

"He just turned four months," Jake said proudly.

"Congratulations," Mr. North said as they climbed up the hill.

"I'd love grandchildren," Mrs. North mused.

"You'll be waiting a while," Kelsey commented.

"You never know. You might find a nice young man to marry," Kelly

North said breezily. Kelsey cringed inside. She could tell by her mother's tone that she had some scheme in mind. Kelsey hoped that it wasn't a blind date.

"Even if I did, I'm not having any kids for a long time," Kelsey replied. Kelly North frowned.

"One milestone at a time. Let's go see you get sworn in," Dan North said comfortingly.

Kelsey beamed as she returned to the office with Jake and her parents an hour later. Her father had taken lots of photos of Kelsey standing in the courtroom, hand raised to take the Oath of Attorney. Kelsey had been pleased to see Judge Aguilar on the bench, along with several other members of the King County Superior Court.

Tyler and Tori had been standing in the front, and Jake and Kelsey had decided to return to the office without waiting for them, in case Tyler and Tori needed to go back to the client's office and continue working on the merger.

Two people who weren't at the swearing-in were Ryan and Jess, who had been sworn in privately at the office of one of Bob's friends, who was a longtime judge. Zach would get sworn in in Bellevue later.

Jake said goodbye to Kelsey and her family as he headed over to Starbucks, and Kelsey led her parents up to the Simon and Associates office.

"Wow, Kels," her dad said, looking around.

"Kelsey. Bill wants to see you," Marie said.

"Thanks," Kelsey replied. "Mom and Dad, this is Marie and Millie. They run everything."

Millie giggled and Marie nodded.

"You got that right," Marie commented.

"I'll take you guys to my office first," Kelsey said to her parents. They walked over to Kelsey's office.

"Have a seat," Kelsey said. "I'll be right back, then we can have dinner." Kelsey walked out of her office and down the hall to Bill's.

"Bill?" she said, walking in.

"Sit," Bill replied, without looking up. Kelsey sat in one of the client chairs, as Bill finished looking over a document.

A moment later, Jake walked in.

"Congratulations to both of you," Bill said, looking at them. "I need the two of you to go home, pack up and get on a plane to Phoenix tonight. Marie has your tickets. I think they're for nine p.m."

"What?" Jake said. "Why?"

"The other side has produced the discovery documents in the Landau case. There's fifty bankers boxes."

"Fifty?" Kelsey asked.

"No way," Jake said.

"I don't see the point of having them trucked up here. We'd have to rent a new space anyway. We'll get a team to help you down there and get it done."

"Kelsey and I are going to stay in Phoenix, Arizona and go through fifty boxes of contracts?" Jake said.

"Yes," Bill replied.

"Bill, I have a new baby," Jake protested.

"You have a wife," Bill replied.

"Send someone else. Send Tyler," Jake said. Kelsey felt her heart skip.

"Tyler's working on something more important. Look, Jake, you can come up on the weekends to visit the baby. I'll pay for it. But I need you to go now," Bill said.

"How long do you think it will take?" Kelsey asked.

"It depends on how efficient you are, Kelsey. Do you need to fly back up?" Bill asked.

"No," Kelsey said.

"Good. Then that's time that won't be wasted. Let me know when you arrive, and we'll set up a conference call in the morning, so you'll know exactly what you're looking for. Have a safe flight."

Kelsey and Jake glanced at each other and walked out of the office toward Marie's desk.

"I'm dead," Jake said. "Sara's going to kill me."

"She'll understand," Kelsey said comfortingly.

"She won't," Jake replied. .

Marie handed each of them an envelope. "Your plane leaves at 9:20. You'll be at the Sheraton. The client is paying for the room, but any extras are on you."

"Is Bill paying for my divorce when I let my wife know I'm leaving her alone with the baby?"

Marie smiled at him. "That's an extra, Jake. Call me if you need anything."

Jake and Kelsey headed back to their offices. Jake looked at the ticket.

"We're in cattle class," he said.

"At least we're in the Sheraton," Kelsey said.

"Small favors," Jake replied, walking into his office. Kelsey walked into hers. Her parents were looking out the window.

"Ready, Kels?" her mother asked, turning.

"Change of plans," Kelsey said. "Can you drive me to Sea-Tac tonight?"

"Beautiful view, Kelsey." her dad said a half-hour later, as he looked at Elliott Bay out of her living room window. "Better than at your office."

"Yeah," Kelsey said.

"Is this place expensive?" he asked.

"More than my last place," Kelsey hedged.

"There's no price to put on your safety," her mom said, kissing Kelsey's forehead. "I'll help you get packed." They walked into Kelsey's bedroom.

"I have no idea what to take," Kelsey said. "I don't know how long I'll be there."

"Just pack a week's worth of clothes. They have stores in Phoenix," her father said.

"Helpful, Dan," his wife said. Kelsey's dad grinned.

"I wonder if you'll be back for Thanksgiving," Kelsey's mother said, opening Kelsey's closet.

"No way. Not with fifty boxes. I'll be lucky to get back for Christmas," Kelsey replied. "And I don't want you two trying to come to Phoenix. I'll be fine."

Kelsey walked over to the closet. She selected five dresses and two suits and put them on the bed.

"Don't forget your exercise stuff," her mom said. "I'm sure you'll want it."

"I will. I hope they have a gym," Kelsey commented.

"The Sheraton? I'm sure they do," her father said, sitting on the bed.

Kelsey placed a stack of exercise clothes on the bed. She added several pairs of PJs and some underwear. Her mother located Kelsey's mini travel bags and began packing.

"What are you going to put all of this in?" she asked.

"I have no idea. I don't own any luggage. I'd call Jess, but I don't think there's enough time."

"We can buy you a carry-on at the airport," her father said. "Just throw it in anything for now."

Kelsey located her backpack, and placed shoes and the neatly-packed clothes inside. Her mother put the dresses into the garment bag Kelsey's wool dress had come in and zipped it up. Kelsey packed the rest of the things she would need in her gym bag, including her work laptop and her Chanel cosmetic bag.

"Is that it? We should go. Then we'll have time to get something to eat at the airport," her father said.

"I think that's all," Kelsey said, looking around.

"Then let's go, Ms. Lawyer," her father said, picking up the backpack.

Kelsey paid too much for a suitcase at the airport, and she and her parents ate dinner at one of the restaurants that was outside of the security entrance.

"Kelsey, those are beautiful pearls," Kelly North said. "May I?" she said, reaching out to touch them.

Kelsey took a deep breath, as her mother touched the necklace. She was wearing the pearls that Tyler had bought for her.

"Are they real?" her mother asked in amazement.

"What time is your flight again?" Kelsey's father interrupted.

Kelsey looked at her father, and realized that he knew that Tyler had given her the necklace.

"9:20," she said, grateful for the distraction. "We should finish up."

Kelly North turned back to her soup, and Kelsey's father gave Kelsey a smile.

Fifteen minutes later, Kelsey gave her parents hugs and said goodbye to them. Then she got into the long line to pass through security. Kelsey couldn't help but look at the empty first class line with longing.

She met up with Jake at the gate, where he was playing a video game on his tablet.

"Why?" he said when he saw her.

Kelsey just shook her head.

At 12:30 a.m. Kelsey's phone rang. She and Jake had just checked into the Sheraton, and Kelsey was getting ready for bed.

"I didn't get to say goodbye," Tyler said softly.

"I know," Kelsey said sadly. She was sorry that she hadn't seen him before she left, particularly since she didn't know when she'd be back in Seattle.

"I wanted to tell you something," Tyler said.

"Tell me now."

"I wanted to tell you in person," Tyler replied. "It will wait. Take care of yourself. I'll miss you."

"I'll miss you too," Kelsey replied. And she knew she would. She already missed his kisses, and now she would miss seeing him every day.

After her run the next morning, Kelsey picked up a coffee at the cafe in the hotel lobby. Carrying the paper cup, she walked over to Jake, who was on his phone as he sat in one of the leather chairs. Jake glanced up.

"Kelsey's here. Yeah. I love you guys too. OK, I'll call you later," Jake said. He hung up the phone and stood up.

"I'm a dead man when I get back," Jake mused.

"You made it onto the plane," Kelsey said, taking a sip of her coffee.

Jake shook his head. "She didn't want to kill me in front of the baby," he said.

"It will be OK," Kelsey said. "Let's go."

Jake nodded. He and Kelsey headed outside, and as Kelsey drank her coffee, the valet arranged for their cab. Kelsey finished the last bit of the warm coffee as the bright green cab pulled up. The valet offered to throw her cup away, and after thanking him, Kelsey followed Jake into the cab.

"You could have walked," the cabby said, looking at the business card that Jake had handed him.

"It's too hot," Jake said, taking the card back. Kelsey glanced at him. Actually it was perfect weather, mid-seventies and sunny. She supposed she wasn't wearing a suit, so maybe Jake had a different perspective. Her short-sleeved shift dress was comfortable.

The cabby shrugged, and they drove off.

Kelsey couldn't help but smile a few minutes later. The cab had basically circled the block. It had been much like the Tactec holiday parties she had previously been to. Jake paid the cabby, and Kelsey got out and enjoyed the desert sun that warmed her face.

"Let's go," Jake said grumpily. Kelsey followed him into the office building, and a cool blast of air greeted them. Jake consulted the card, hit the elevator button and they headed upstairs.

A few minutes later, the two of them were sitting in a conference room looking out over downtown Phoenix. Glasses of water were in front of them, and Kelsey had her phone out, ready to take notes. She knew from experience that Jake would ask her questions about the meeting later. He wasn't much of a listener.

"So how's Bill Simon?" their host asked, sitting down at the table. A slightly pudgy lawyer with a nice smile, Roger Morang had greeted them at the door. It was 8 a.m., and a little early for a receptionist to be in the office.

"He's good," Kelsey offered.

"Still working a million hours a week?" Roger asked knowingly.

"Yes," Jake replied.

"How long have you two been there?"

"August," Kelsey replied.

"And how long are you planning on staying? I won't tell," Roger said conspiratorially.

"At least until next week," Jake quipped.

"Probably the right attitude," Roger said seriously. "All right. Bill's calling in a few minutes, but here's what I know right now. Fifty boxes of documents are being unloaded as we speak. I've hired a temporary to help you work on this, and I've also called the dean over at the law school, and he's arranging for some of the work-study students to come over and help the three of you."

"Where are we working?" Jake asked. "Here?"

Roger shook his head. "I've arranged for the boardroom over at the Sheraton. You'll have 24-hour access."

"Great," Kelsey said. She was impressed that Roger had managed to organize everything for them so quickly, considering that the documents had arrived yesterday afternoon.

"Wonderful," Jake said with less enthusiasm.

"The faster you're done, the faster you can get home," Roger pointed out.

"True," Jake said.

"You have a kid, right?" Roger asked.

"I do."

"Then you'll want to hurry and get back," Roger commented as the phone rang. "Hello, Bill," he said.

"Roger. Are Kelsey and Jake with you?" Bill asked over the speakerphone.

"We're here," Kelsey replied.

"Hey, Bill," Jake said wearily.

"All right, you two, I've emailed both of you a list of the types of things that we're looking for. Roger's going to drop by every so often to make sure that you're on the right track, but Kelsey's in charge."

"Of course," Jake said under his breath, but Kelsey knew that he didn't care. In fact, he was probably pleased, because it would mean less work for him.

"Kelsey, you can set the hours for the two of you. As long as you're billing at least ten hours a day each, I don't care."

Jake groaned softly. Billing ten hours meant that they would probably be working thirteen or more daily. Kelsey didn't particularly mind. Although the weather was great, she wanted to get back to Seattle too. And, although she was a tiny bit reluctant to admit it, back to Tyler.

"Just make sure that you're keeping all of the documents under lock and key. Everyone will need to sign a non-disclosure agreement. I've sent that to you as well."

"I've printed a stack for you," Roger said.

"Thanks," Kelsey said to him.

"That's it. Call me if you have any questions, and I want to see what you find on a daily basis."

"OK," Kelsey said. "But what about our other cases?" With fifty boxes to go through, Kelsey knew that they would likely be in Arizona for at least a couple of weeks.

"Tyler and I will hold down the fort for a while. I'll let you know if Samson settles. Roger, thanks for keeping an eye on them."

"I'm sure they'll be fine," Roger said pleasantly.

"I've got a meeting. Keep me in the loop," Bill said. "Talk to you later."

"Bye, Bill," Kelsey said. Roger and Jake said their goodbyes, and Bill disconnected.

"Any questions?" Roger asked kindly.

Kelsey and Jake shook their heads.

"I'll walk you back over to the hotel. The temp will be there at nine, and the boxes should all be there by now," Roger said.

"Walk?" Jake whispered doubtfully to Kelsey.

Faster than the morning's taxi ride, the trio walked back into the air-conditioned comfort of the Sheraton. Roger led them up to the second floor and into a spacious boardroom. Two women were there, sitting at the table, a key on the table in front of them. Boxes, stacked three high, lined two of the walls.

"They're done?"

"Yes," one of the women said, as she stood.

"I hope you weren't waiting long."

"Ten minutes," the other woman said, rising and taking the key from the table.

"Kelsey and Jake, this is Janine and Mary, two of the secretaries from my office," Roger said, taking the key.

Everyone greeted each other, and Roger handed Kelsey the key.

"Kelsey, there are a few staff people that had the keys to the room, but the hotel manager should have collected them by now. He'll drop by to verify that with you, and when he does, have him sign an NDA. While you're here, he'll be the only one with access to this room. I'll stick around until the temp arrives, and I'll come back later this afternoon when the law students arrive around three."

"Did you need us for anything else?" one of the secretaries asked.

"I think we're all set," Roger replied.

"It was nice to meet you," she said to Jake and Kelsey. Everyone said their goodbyes, and the secretaries left.

Within the half-hour, a very good-looking temporary worker named Samuel arrived at the boardroom. After he signed the NDA and Roger explained the case to him, Roger left the group to allow them to get organized.

By eleven, Kelsey had a plan to go through the boxes. Samuel, who had blue eyes that rivaled Ryan's — and Jake, who had shed his suit jacket — had moved several of the boxes, and had started thumbing through them to get a sense of the types of documents that they would be tackling. Kelsey had called Roger once, to find out if the law students could work on weekends. He had assured her that the hours for the students were flexible, but that Samuel was limited to 9 to 5 during the week, so they wouldn't have to pay overtime.

"No overtime for us," Jake commented, his eyes scanning a old contract.

"You should be used to it," Kelsey commented, pulling up her calculator on her phone. Roger had assured her that she would have a minimum of five students, although he couldn't assure her that they would all be good at document reviewing.

"I will never be used to it," Jake replied. Kelsey focused on her phone as she punched in some numbers. Assuming everyone worked out, and that the documents that she had seen were representative, she calculated that they would be here for at least 20 work days. She sighed to herself. She hoped that the Sheraton served a nice Thanksgiving dinner.

At three, Roger returned, and over the next hour, six law students wandered in. Once again, NDAs were signed, and Roger gave the overview of the case. Then Kelsey had each of the students give her their preferred work schedule. As she expected, there were no early risers in the group.

After a bit of discussion, she and Jake decided that he would open the Arizona office of Simon and Associates at 7 a.m., and Kelsey would close it at 10 p.m., to allow the night owl students to work late. Kelsey would take over on weekends so Jake could visit his family, and she would be there to supervise from 11 to 7. Kelsey figured that she could miss a few Sundays off to get home faster.

The team left, promising to return the next day, and Kelsey and Jake sat in the boardroom, and began to systematically review a box of documents.

"Do you think we'll get home for Christmas?" Jake asked. Kelsey wasn't sure if he was kidding.

"You will. I'm not letting you miss your son's first Christmas," Kelsey replied.

"You could go up on the weekends too. There's no reason to sacrifice yourself."

"I know, but I'd rather just get this done," Kelsey replied. After the team had left, she had removed the pins from her hair, and she brushed her hand through the platinum-blonde strands.

"At least it looks like it's a good group," Jake mused, turning a page in the document he was looking at.

"I hope so," Kelsey said. "I don't want to have to fire anyone."

"Just pretend you're Bill Simon. He fires Tyler every day."

Kelsey laughed. It was true.

"Poor Tyler. He's got to do all of our work," Jake said.

"Yeah, I wonder how that's going to be," Kelsey wondered. Tyler was already working 70+ hour weeks.

"I bet they'll get some postponements," Jake commented.

"That's probably true too," Kelsey agreed. At least a few of her cases could be put on hold for a few weeks until she returned. That was one nice thing about intellectual property. No one's life was on the line, although plenty of money was.

That night, Kelsey crashed into the soft pillows in her room. The lights of downtown Phoenix sparkled outside. She was glad she liked the Sheraton, since it looked like she would be spending most of the rest of November there, going from her room to the second floor, with the occasional trip to the gym or pool. After a late-night call with Bill Simon, Kelsey had managed to get him to spring for meals for her and Jake. She knew that Jake would appreciate the opportunity not to have spend downtown prices for food every day, and of course, she didn't mind saving money either.

She picked up her phone and sent Tyler a message. She missed him already.

How's it going? she asked.

You can imagine, Tyler replied.

I can, Kelsey typed.

When are you coming back?

No time soon.

How many boxes were there?

Fifty, Kelsey replied.

Kelsey felt like there was a slightly longer pause before Tyler replied.

You know what I want to say, right? he asked. And she did. But Kelsey also knew that Tyler's messages weren't private. It was one of the problems with being the scion of a technology guru. The limitation, Kelsey had discovered while dating him, was the reason that Tyler rarely messaged his personal feelings. There was someone at Tactec who could access them all.

The same thing I do, Kelsey replied.

Good. Then I'll talk to you tomorrow, Tyler replied.

Tomorrow, Mr. Olsen, Kelsey replied. And she put her phone on the nightstand and turned out the light.

Kelsey lay in bed until the leisurely hour of nine. Jake had messaged her to let her know that he had retrieved a second key from the manager, and that Samuel had arrived on time. Kelsey enjoyed her run at the gym, then returned to her room to take a shower.

Although she had suggested that Jake leave his suits in his room and dress in business casual wear for the rest of the project, Kelsey wore her usual outfit — a classic dress and heels. She felt that, as the designated supervisor, she needed to present a professional appearance, particularly with the law students. At 10:50, she left her room and headed downstairs.

It didn't take long for the group to find a rhythm as they were working together. Samuel, in addition to his soft blue eyes and sexy grin, had a wicked sense of humor and a serious work ethic. Jake, who was focused on getting back to Seattle as quickly as possible, worked with an intensity that was usually rare for him in Simon's office. And of course, Kelsey worked steadily and with her usual determination.

The law students joined them during the afternoon, and Kelsey found herself switching from reviewing documents, to supervising others. She didn't have a lot of supervisory experience, but she supposed that she would learn on the job.

People came and went as needed, and by 9:30 p.m., Kelsey sat in the room alone. The day had been productive, but Kelsey couldn't help but think it had been slow-going. They had managed to go through a total of one box. She hoped that they would speed up over time — otherwise, she might be lucky to return to Seattle for Christmas herself.

She called Simon's office to give him an update, but to her surprise, Tyler answered the call.

"Tyler?" Kelsey asked, upon hearing his voice.

"Hey, Kels."

"I was supposed to update Bill," she said.

"You have the pleasure of updating me instead," Tyler replied. "Simon went to a bar meeting."

Kelsey smiled. "Well, that is a pleasure," she replied.

"Are you flirting with me, Miss North?" Tyler asked. Kelsey could hear the smile in his voice.

"Absolutely not," she replied, as seriously as she could.

"Well, that's a disappointment," Tyler replied.

"You are trouble, Mr. Olsen."

"I hope so," Tyler replied. "Did you find anything?"

"Nope," Kelsey replied.

"But you're almost done?" Tyler asked hopefully.

"Tyler, we got through one box," Kelsey replied.

"At that rate, you won't be back until next year."

"Don't I know it."

"Speed it up," Tyler ordered.

Kelsey laughed. "Yes, sir," she teased.

"I mean it. Bill shouldn't have sent you down there anyway. He should have had the boxes shipped up here."

"You told him that, didn't you?" Kelsey asked.

"Of course I did. He said that he wanted the two of you to focus without distractions. So he's forcing Jake's family to be without him, and me to be without you."

Kelsey's heart skipped. "Do you miss me?"

"You know I do," Tyler replied.

"I miss you too," Kelsey said.

"So hurry up. Toss some of the boxes out of the window. Pretend they only delivered ten, and come home next week."

Kelsey giggled. "I'll see what I can do."

"No, you won't. You'll be diligent, and you'll let me miss you. You won't be back until you've done a good job for the client."

"Is that a bad thing?"

"It is for me," Tyler replied.

"For me too. But I'll come home soon."

"You'll come home to me?" Tyler asked hopefully.

"I will," Kelsey said solemnly.

Kelsey thought after she hung up the phone with Tyler. She leaned back in the dark leather swivel chair and stretched out her bare legs under the wooden table. She sat there and had the same thought that she had been thinking for weeks. The question of whether she was kidding herself.

She knew Tyler, and she knew him well enough to know that he wasn't giving her up. It was clear with every word, and every glance. But what Kelsey couldn't figure out was what giving up meant for him.

Would they be like this for years? Working with each other? Flirting whenever no one else was in the room or listening on the phone?

Kelsey accepted that she had agreed to Tyler's terms. He had offered to fight for her, and she had agreed.

But Kelsey had never been patient. An hour felt long to her. Whereas Tyler seemed to think in months, if not years.

Kelsey still didn't understand why he had turned down Lisa's dinner invitation. The CEO of Tactec had held out an olive branch after sidelining him for six months, and Tyler had acted as if he had seen her last week. Nonchalant, as if the gesture didn't matter.

But Kelsey knew that it did. Lisa knew she and Tyler worked in the same office, for the same attorney, on the same projects. Could Lisa be naive enough to believe that they no longer cared about each other? Kelsey didn't believe that for a minute.

But perhaps she was distracted enough that she didn't realize how much they meant to each other, even now, even after Lisa had ordered both of them to end their relationship. Kelsey knew from the media that Lisa Olsen had plenty of things to think about. And Kelsey wouldn't be surprised at all that her son Tyler wasn't at the top of the list.

Maybe Tyler understood that too. He had mentioned it when he refused the invitation. He had said that he didn't have enough leverage for Lisa to listen to him, and he was going to wait until he did.

Kelsey sighed and turned the chair to face the near wall of boxes. Maybe it was good that she was here, far away from Seattle. But she hated being far away from Tyler.

After a couple of days, Kelsey had sized up the students from the local law school. Rhian, a girl with dark brown hair and a bright smile, was the most Type-A of the group, and reminded Kelsey of herself. Leo was her laid-back opposite, usually coming into the boardroom wearing shorts and flip-flops. Jordan was a petite, punky redhead, with a lot of attitude, but the smarts to back it up. Thom was a sport fanatic who always wore a jersey of some sort, with a matching ball cap. Michael was a chatty jokester and Paloma was a quiet, diligent worker. Kelsey felt lucky to have all of them, because although it was an interesting mix of students, they were all very focused and ready to work.

By the time that the weekend had rolled around, Kelsey felt more positive about everything in her life, including the boxes that filled the boardroom. On Sunday, they had managed to plow through two full boxes, despite the fact that both Jake and Sam were away. Kelsey wondered if the pizzas that she had ordered for the law students had helped. If that was the case, she'd be ordering them every weekend. Perhaps every day.

It also helped that instead of sitting in the boardroom, Kelsey was sitting in a lounge chair, by the edge of the pool of the Sheraton. She had taken a swim, and she was enjoying the sun.

Her phone buzzed and Kelsey reached out for it with her hand. She opened her eyes, and grinned when she saw the caller.

"Hi, Jess. How are you?"

"Great, but I should be asking you. How's it going?" Jessica replied.

"Slow," Kelsey admitted. "But we're getting it done. How's Seattle?"

"Rainy and overcast. Be glad you're there," Jessica replied. "Will you be back for Thanksgiving?"

Kelsey sighed.

"Bill offered to fly me up, but I think I'd rather stay here. I can probably get a few boxes done over the break."

"Well, you'll have some help. Ryan and I are going to come down. If we're invited, that is."

"Of course you're invited!" Kelsey said excitedly. "But you don't have to work."

"It will be good for us. We don't do anything at Tactec," Jessica said breezily. "We'll fly down on Wednesday and stay until Sunday. Can you take any time off? Besides dinner?"

"For you I can," Kelsey said.

"Cool, then maybe we can take a day trip," Jess said. "How's the Sheraton?"

"It's great. I'm sitting by the pool now."

"OK, that was really mean," Jessica said.

Kelsey laughed. "Sorry," she said.

"Maybe I shouldn't have been so quick to dismiss moving to California when Ryan suggested it," Jessica mused. "I'll have Carol make the reservations tomorrow. Do you want us to bring anything down?"

"Just yourselves," Kelsey said happily.

"I'm so excited to see you. I miss you so much," Jessica said.

"Me too. So everything's OK up there?"

"Yeah," Jessica said, but there was a bit of a faraway tone in her voice.

"What's going on?" Kelsey asked.

"Ryan's acting strange," Jessica mused.

"Yeah, you're going to have to explain what you mean by that," Kelsey teased gently.

Jessica laughed. "Well, you know how he was seeing Tyler most weekends?"

"Sure," Kelsey replied.

"Well, Ryan was home last weekend, but twice he cancelled lunch."

"OK," Kelsey said.

"Twice in a week," Jessica clarified. "And he wouldn't tell me why."

"That's strange," Kelsey agreed. Ryan always had lunch with Jessica. And she couldn't imagine why he wouldn't tell Jessica if he couldn't.

"He said he had some errands to run for Tyler, but he wouldn't say what he was doing," Jessica said.

Kelsey sighed. She understood perfectly. Tyler was full of secrets lately too.

"I don't understand what's gotten into him," Jessica said. "As soon as Tyler started talking to him again, it's like Ryan doesn't have a life of his own anymore. He's always doing Tyler's bidding."

Kelsey felt like Jessica was exaggerating a bit, but she knew what Jess meant. After months of Tyler not talking to Ryan, it was strange that suddenly they were best friends.

"Anyway, maybe I'll get my husband back when we're in Arizona," Jessica mused.

"We'll have fun," Kelsey said positively.

One of the small perks of being in Arizona was the fact that Kelsey's morning began not only with her usual run, but also with at least an hour by the pool. Occasionally, Kelsey felt a twinge of guilt for refusing to look at her emails before 10 a.m., but she reminded herself that it was rare for her to fall into her hotel bed before midnight. She had shifted her work from early mornings in Seattle to late nights in Arizona.

Bill, and she suspected Tyler, were keeping both her and Jake's inboxes relatively clear of incoming work, so they could focus on finding the documents that they had been sent down here to discover. Thanks to the fact that he had the early shift, Jake was spending his evening hours on Skype, watching his son have dinner, as Jake ate his own dinner over a thousand miles away. Kelsey, on the other hand, was taking advantage of the opportunity for a bit of self-care, after months of living at work.

Kelsey was super motivated over the next few days when she was working. She knew that with Jess and Ryan in town, she would want to spend time hanging out with them instead of going through contracts, so she pushed herself to get as much done as she could. But she still made time to go to the pool first thing in the morning.

"So what are you doing for Thanksgiving?" Samuel asked Kelsey as he was leaving on Wednesday afternoon. It was a week to the day since they had started the project, and the two of them were the only ones in the room. Jake had left for Seattle, and all of the students were heading back to their respective homes for the holiday. "Jake said you were staying."

"My friends are flying down tonight," Kelsey said, pushing a strand of blonde hair out of her eyes.

"Oh, too bad," Samuel said.

"Too bad?" Kelsey asked.

"I was going to invite you to spend the holiday with me," Samuel commented causally. Kelsey looked at him in surprise. Samuel's words had been completely unexpected. "I'm heading home," he added.

"I see. Well, thank you," Kelsey said. She was slightly puzzled.

"Have a good vacation, Kelsey," Samuel said.

"You too," Kelsey said, and he left.

Kelsey only allowed herself a few minutes to think about Samuel after he left. She supposed he was just being kind, since he knew that she was here alone. Kelsey put it out of her mind, and turned her attention back to the contracts in front of her. She was hoping to finish before Ryan and Jess arrived this evening.

At 7:30, Kelsey's phone buzzed, and she picked it up excitedly.

"Where are you?" Jessica asked.

"My room," Kelsey replied. She had left the boardroom a half-hour earlier, to have time to take a shower and change.

"We'll be right there. We're down the hall," Jessica said, and she disconnected. Less than a minute later, there was a knock on Kelsey's door.

"Kelsey!" Jessica said, giving her a hug after Kelsey opened it.

"Hey, Kels," Ryan said, hugging Kelsey as well.

"Thanks for coming," Kelsey said. She looked at Jessica's face. Jess was glowing.

"This is for you," Jessica said, handing Kelsey a bag, which Kelsey knew held designer goods.

"Thank you," Kelsey said, taking it. There was no point in complaining.

"This is nice too," Ryan said, walking around Kelsey's room and looking out at the view.

"You're all checked in?" Kelsey asked.

"We are. It was such a quick trip from the airport," Jessica said, sitting down in the chair next to Kelsey's bed.

"Are you still tired?" Ryan asked. Jessica nodded, and Ryan looked a little worried.

"Maybe you need to go to the doctor," Ryan commented.

"Stop nagging," Jessica said.

"Are you OK?" Kelsey asked.

"Just a little under the weather," Jessica said. "I'll be fine."

"OK," Kelsey said, but like Ryan she wasn't comforted by Jessica's words. She looked at Jessica again.

"Let's eat," Jessica said with determination, lifting herself out of the chair. "Where should we go?"

The trio headed to a Mexican cantina a few blocks from the hotel.

"Is Tyler OK?" Kelsey asked Ryan after they ordered. She registered Jessica's frown, but ignored it. Kelsey assumed that Ryan had seen Tyler, and she had to admit she was a little worried about him and how he was holding up doing her work and Jake's.

"Tyler is in his little Tyler cocoon," Ryan said to Kelsey. "I haven't seen him for two weeks."

Kelsey saw Jessica look at Ryan. So the errands he had run for Tyler hadn't involved Ryan seeing him.

"Tyler told Jeffrey he was going to work all weekend and wouldn't be in Medina for dinner."

"On Thanksgiving?" Kelsey asked. But she reminded herself, Tyler was refusing to see Lisa Olsen these days.

"You're working too," Jessica pointed out.

Kelsey laughed. "Yeah, I guess so."

"Bill Simon is a nightmare," Ryan commented.

"He's fine. He just expects you to work hard," Kelsey replied.

"When are you coming back?" Ryan asked. "We miss you."

"I miss you guys too," Kelsey said. "But we still have a lot of boxes to get through."

"Tyler said you had fifty?" Ryan asked.

"There's forty now," Kelsey replied.

"Will you get back for Christmas?" Ryan asked in concern.

"I think so," Kelsey replied. "It's going pretty well."

"I can't believe that Bill Simon sent you guys down here," Jessica said.

"It's fine," Kelsey shrugged as her lime drink arrived.

"Tyler misses you," Ryan commented nonchalantly. Jessica glared at him. Kelsey didn't comment.

She missed Tyler too.

Over the next four days, Kelsey, Jess, and Ryan hung out together. They took a helicopter flight over the Grand Canyon, which was spectacular. Kelsey took them to some of the nicest restaurants that Phoenix had to offer, and they actually managed to finish another few boxes of paperwork.

Jessica was irritable during the entire weekend, although she didn't seem upset with Ryan, or with anything in particular. She just seemed a little fussy. Perhaps she was right, and was coming down with a cold.

But Kelsey had a feeling that something else was going on. However, since Ryan was always with them, she never had an opportunity to ask Jessica alone.

Jess and Ryan returned to Seattle on Sunday night, and Kelsey decided to spend the last moments of her long weekend next to the pool. She was wearing a new bikini, courtesy of Mrs. Ryan Perkins, who had required everyone to go shopping with her. When they had, Jess bought numerous summer clothes that she wouldn't be able to wear in Seattle until July, including a half dozen maxi sundresses.

Kelsey's phone rang. It was Tyler.

"Hi, Tyler."

"Done yet?" he asked in greeting.

"No," Kelsey replied.

Tyler sighed. "Hurry," he said.

"How was your Thanksgiving?" Kelsey asked, smiling.

"Uneventful," Tyler replied.

"You didn't see Lisa."

"I did not," Tyler replied.

Kelsey bit her lip. She couldn't help but wonder what was going on with Tyler, but she felt she shouldn't ask.

Everyone was back to work on Monday. To Kelsey's surprise, Jake seemed relaxed. It turned out that he had had a long talk with his wife, and she had accepted that he was working away from them so he could provide for her and the baby, despite the fact that she was still unhappy about it.

Samuel, on the other hand, seemed distracted. Kelsey wondered how his vacation had been, but she didn't know him well enough to pry.

By the 1st of December, Kelsey had a glimmer of hope. They still hadn't found what they were looking for, but the group was steadily working through the boxes, and if they managed to keep up the pace, Kelsey was confident that she would be back in Seattle for Christmas. She had talked to Morgan, and decided that she would make a point of returning to Port Townsend for at least a few days for a visit. Bill Simon closed the office for the last two weeks of the year, so Kelsey wouldn't need to return until January 2nd, although she knew that she probably would be back in her apartment before the new year. Despite the fact that her current truce with her mother was still holding, there was no guarantee that it would last. Anyway, Grandma Rose was planning on coming for a visit. That alone would probably destroy the peace.

Kelsey spoke to both Bill and Tyler on most days of the week. She spoke to Bill to update him, and to Tyler to get an update. As she had expected, most of her cases had been extended, although Tyler had written a few pleadings in her absence.

Kelsey missed Tyler, and more than once he had expressed that he missed her too. She knew from his comments that he was working at least fifteen-hour days, and she suspected that since she wasn't around to question him, he was working most Sundays as well. She didn't feel like she could judge, as she was doing the same.

On Saturday evening, Kelsey was pleased to have a short break. They were close, she could feel it.

Kelsey walked down the street, cardigan around her shoulders. It was dark, but there were plenty of sparkling lights on the street, and happy tourists and couples were taking advantage of the festive holiday spirit.

Kelsey had stopped by the hotel cafe and got a peppermint mocha, which she held in her hands to gently warm them. It wasn't cold by Seattle standards, but Kelsey had grown accustomed to Phoenix's warm days, and the nights were beginning to seem chilly. She wondered what it would feel like when she returned to the Pacific Northwest.

She took a sip of her drink, then stopped abruptly. Focused on her coffee, she had almost bumped into one of the holiday couples that were around her.

"Sorry," Kelsey said, looking up. She gasped softly in surprise. In front of her was Bob Perkins, but the other half of the hand-holding couple wasn't Morgan Hill.

"It's OK," said the tall, striking woman with long warm caramel-blonde hair. Kelsey looked at Bob, who looked as surprised to see her as she was to see him.

"Kelsey," Bob said, and the woman looked over at Bob. Kelsey guessed that she was about the same age as Bob, although like Bob, she didn't look her age.

"Hi, Bob," Kelsey managed to say. The woman raised an eyebrow.

"Fiona," Bob said, "this is Ryan's roommate from Darrow. Kelsey, this is Fiona."

Kelsey watched as the woman visibly relaxed and stuck out her hand. Kelsey shook Fiona's hand, which was perfectly manicured and flaunted a diamond ring, although not on her ring finger.

Kelsey's mind raced as they stood awkwardly in the middle of the block. This was the woman Tyler had told her about long ago, the woman that Bob had been seeing in Arizona well before he met Morgan. Kelsey was sure of it.

"It's lovely to meet one of Ryan's friends," Fiona said. "I've heard so much about him."

The words were interesting. Fiona hadn't met Ryan. It was puzzling, because if Kelsey was right, and this was Bob's Arizona girlfriend, she had known Bob for years. Yet she hadn't met Bob's son?

"Bill had mentioned that you were here," Bob said. "Are you almost done with your project?"

"Soon, I hope," Kelsey said, continuing to scan Fiona, as Fiona looked at Bob. She was beautiful, with green eyes, a slim figure, and an ample chest. Kelsey recognized the impeccable tailoring of the luxurious designer clothes she wore, and her nose caught just a hint of Fiona's expensive perfume.

"Fantastic," Bob said, and Kelsey could tell that he was trying to extract himself from the delicate situation that he found himself in. "We've got a reservation, so we'd better get going," he said, as if the restaurant wouldn't hold a table for billionaire Bob Perkins.

"We'd be happy to have you join us," Fiona chimed in, to both Kelsey and Bob's visible surprise. "I'd love to get to know one of Ryan's friends."

Kelsey paused before answering. For a moment, she considered accepting, so as to discover more about the woman who was clearly Morgan's rival for Bob's affection. But Kelsey realized that Fiona would be likely to steer the conversation to her preferred topic, Bob's family.

"I'm sorry," Kelsey said, declining. "I have some errands to run. Thank you though."

"Next time, then," Bob said, and Kelsey thought she noted a sigh of relief.

"Sure," Kelsey said as brightly as she could. "It was nice to meet you. Have a wonderful dinner."

"Thank you," Fiona said, giving Bob's arm a squeeze.

"Goodbye, Kelsey," Bob said, and he and Fiona walked on.

Kelsey glanced back at the couple and pulled her sweater over her shoulders.

Now what was she going to do?

Kelsey returned to her room at the Sheraton an hour later. She put her bag from the bookstore in the armchair and got into her lounge pants and long-sleeved Portland State shirt. Kelsey shoved the bag onto the floor as she climbed into the armchair and pulled her legs into the seat. She reached down into the bag and pulled out the local running magazine that she had bought. She opened it, but didn't look down at the words.

Kelsey wasn't sure what came next. Did she tell Morgan that the woman that Morgan already knew about was on a date with Bob? Did Morgan know? Would she care?

Kelsey knew that Morgan had seen what Fiona looked like, because Morgan had admitted to looking her up on Google, so Kelsey had little to add. She had been too surprised to register anything much besides the fact that Fiona seemed pleasant enough, although perhaps a bit possessive. That was clear from her reaction when Bob had first seen Kelsey. Perhaps Fiona knew about Morgan too.

After a while, there was a knock on Kelsey's door. She stood up, and looked out of the peephole. Bob was standing outside, and Kelsey opened the door. A part of her wasn't surprised that he was there.

"Hi, Kelsey," Bob said to her. "May I come in?"

"Of course," Kelsey said. Bob walked in, and Kelsey closed the door behind him. Bob sat in the chair that Kelsey had just vacated. He was still wearing the suit he had worn with Fiona.

Bob glanced at Kelsey, who sat cross-legged on her bed.

"Well, that was awkward," Bob commented, smiling at her. But Kelsey didn't smile back. She wanted to know where Morgan stood in all of this, and she was waiting to find out. Bob seemed to understand, and nodded thoughtfully.

"I'll tell Morgan that Fiona and I ran into you. I'll ask Morgan to mention it to you."

"OK," Kelsey said. She waited to see if Bob had anything else to say. Kelsey didn't.

"LIfe is complicated, Kelsey," Bob said thoughtfully. "I know you understand that."

"I just care about Morgan," Kelsey replied.

"I know. I do too," Bob said.

Then why are you going out with Fiona? Kelsey thought, but didn't ask.

Bob stood up and brushed off his pants.

"Good luck with your project," Bob said. "Bill said you're doing great."

"Thank you," Kelsey said. She thought she should stand out of politeness, but she couldn't bring herself to be polite. She was too upset for Morgan.

"Have a good night, Kelsey," Bob said.

"Good night, Bob," Kelsey said. Bob looked at Kelsey for a long moment. Then he sighed.

He walked over to the door and left.

The next morning, Kelsey woke to the sound of her phone. She glanced at the readout.

Morgan.

"Hi," Kelsey said, a bit sleepily.

"Hey, babe," Morgan said. "Did I wake you?"

"It's fine," Kelsey said, sitting up. "I should have gotten up an hour ago."

"Bob told me that you met Fiona," Morgan said in a rush.

"I did. Last night."

"That must have been terrible for you," Morgan said.

"It was. I didn't know how I was going to tell you," Kelsey admitted.

"It's fine, Kels. I knew he was there," Morgan said.

"Good," Kelsey said.

"What's she like?" Morgan asked.

Kelsey thought for a moment. Although she had only been in Fiona's presence for a short moment, Kelsey knew that Morgan would want to know any and everything that she could think of.

"I know she's pretty," Morgan added.

"Yes, she is."

"And old," Morgan said cattily.

Kelsey giggled. "Morgan," she scolded.

"Just sayin'. What else?"

"She dresses beautifully, and I liked her perfume. She's well put together."

"Not a surprise," Morgan said. "What else?"

"She hasn't met Ryan," Kelsey said.

"That's a surprise," Morgan said.

"I thought so too," Kelsey agreed. "She invited me to dinner, I think so she could find out more about him."

"Really? You should have gone," Morgan said.

"I didn't think I could have gotten through dinner," Kelsey said. "It was too weird."

"Yeah, I could see that," Morgan agreed. "Anything else?"

"Not really. I only saw them for a minute."

"What was Bob like with her?" Morgan asked. And Kelsey paused. She wasn't sure if she should lie to Morgan or not. But Kelsey decided that Morgan needed to know the truth.

"Happy," Kelsey said softly and she waited for Morgan to respond.

Morgan sighed into the phone.

"I figured," she said.

"I'm sorry," Kelsey said.

"It's not your fault. It's not his," Morgan replied. "It just is."

"Does this change things for you?" Kelsey asked her.

"No," Morgan said. "Sadly, it doesn't."

Kelsey wasn't sure what to say or if she could say anything. Like Bob had said, life was complicated. And Kelsey knew that Morgan's relationship with Bob was as well.

"What are you doing today?" Kelsey asked.

"I'm going home," Morgan said. "I need to give Carly some money so she can have the car fixed. I figured I'd do some laundry while I was over there. You know Anna can't be bothered. How about you? What will you do today?"

"Go for a run. Hope that we find the smoking gun this week, so maybe I can get back to Seattle this year."

"I hope so. We miss you," Morgan said softly.

"I miss you guys too," Kelsey said.

"Thank you for looking out for me," Morgan said.

"Always," Kelsey replied.

"Take care, Kels," Morgan said. "Love you."

"Love you too, Morgan," Kelsey said, and they disconnected.

As Kelsey ran toward Encanto Park a half hour later, a torrent of thoughts rushed through her mind. Morgan's relationship with Bob, Bob's relationship with Ryan. Ryan's relationship with Tyler, and of course Tyler's relationship with her.

How could Bob have a multi-year relationship with someone who hadn't met his only child? How did Morgan continue to have a relationship with someone in a serious relationship with another woman? What was Ryan plotting with Tyler, and why wasn't he telling his wife, who seemed to have a secret of her own? And of course, why was Tyler so quiet?

At this moment, Kelsey missed her old self. The one who could tune out the world and pretend that nothing mattered, that as long as she was happy, that the world was happy too. Of course, that Kelsey was always miserable.

For the past week, Kelsey had been able to put a lot of these questions out of her mind. But now they were flooding back. And Kelsey had no answers. Only more questions.

On Monday night, Kelsey lay in bed reading her news alerts, and she was a little surprised to see that Tactec's new CFO was the top news from the company. Of course, thanks to Jess, Kelsey had known about the new hire for weeks, but Tactec had just announced it to the press today.

A less reported-on story was Rick Burton's impromptu press conference where he doubled down on his criticisms of Lisa Olsen's management style. Kelsey read the transcript, and despite her own issues with Ms. Olsen, she thought that he was being completely unfair. Rick Burton had called her "unreasonable", "incompetent", and suggested that "she needed to find a man" to improve her personality. The only 'positive' comment he made was his quote, "at least she's attractive".

Kelsey wanted to throw her iPad across the room. Here was a guy whose small startup company had been bought by the multi-billion Tactec, which was created out of thin air because of Lisa Olsen's vision, and he had the nerve to critique her competence. Kelsey had no doubt that Ms. Olsen took such comments with a grain of salt, since Kelsey knew from reading her news feed that rocks were thrown at Lisa Olsen every day, and many of them were focused on her gender. However, Kelsey was outraged.

Kelsey knew that the tech world was largely male and not diverse, much like the legal profession. One thing that she had noticed in her reading though, was that unlike the legal profession — which seemed to understand that they had a diversity problem and needed to take steps to address it — it seemed like the rampant sexism in the tech world was a badge of honor, at least for some people like Rick Burton.

Kelsey wondered what this would mean for her career in the long term. Intellectual property wasn't limited to the tech world, but many, if not most of her clients were likely to come from that world if she continued to focus on software licensing. Would she be able to find companies that wouldn't assume that a female lawyer would be less likely to understand the technology that they wanted to license to other companies? Or should Kelsey reconsider her focus? She hated the idea of backing down from a fight, but she didn't want to hurt her own interests by ignoring the realities of the industry.

Kelsey sighed. No wonder Lisa Olsen had started her own company.

On Wednesday, Kelsey and Jake left Samuel in charge and headed down to the lobby for an attorney meeting.

Jake drank an iced coffee while Kelsey sipped whipped cream off her hot cocoa.

"How can you drink that? It's eighty degrees."

"I like cocoa," Kelsey replied. Jake smiled at her.

"Here we are, the Arizona branch of Simon and Associates. Week four," he said.

"We'll be done soon," Kelsey said soothingly.

Jake looked at her doubtfully.

"OK, before Christmas."

"Always the optimist," he said, taking a drink of coffee and biting a piece of ice.

"Someone's got to be, and it's certainly not going to be you."

"It certainly isn't," Jake replied.

Kelsey laughed. "I did call this meeting for a reason," she commented.

"I thought you called it so I could complain."

"You can do that too. Just let me tell you what Bill asked me to share."

"We're being sent to Indonesia next?" Jake guessed. "Bill has a client there with a thousand boxes?"

"China, and two thousand," Kelsey teased.

"Nothing would surprise me at this point," Jake said grumpily.

"This is good news," Kelsey said.

"Let's hear it," Jake said.

"Bill's decided to give us bonuses for every week we're down here."

"Really? That is good news," Jake said, sitting up.

"He said that he had expected that we would have found the documents by now."

"Does he blame us?"

Kelsey shook her head.

"No, he understands that the documents aren't in any order. He said that he thought that we'd be down here for a maximum of two weeks, and he wants to reward us for sticking it out."

"Great. I wonder if they'll include the bonus in the spousal support award."

Kelsey looked at Jake curiously.

"In my upcoming divorce."

"I thought you said Sara had forgiven you."

"She thought I was going to be down here for a maximum of two weeks too."

Kelsey remembered that Jake had mentioned that Sara had been upset that Jake had to return to Arizona after Thanksgiving.

"Sorry."

"It's fine. Unless we're really going to China."

"Not today," Kelsey said with a grin.

"So what are you doing for Christmas?" Jessica asked. It was eleven p.m., and Kelsey was winding down from another day of work.

"Going home. I hope."

"You couldn't possibly still be there at Christmas, right?"

"I'm just nervous because our students go on Christmas break on the sixteenth. If they aren't done by then, I'm going to be stuck down here finishing up," Kelsey replied.

"OK, that's ridiculous," Jess said.

"I agree, so I'm hoping it doesn't happen. Have you and Ryan decided what you're going to do?"

"I think we're going to L.A. Do you want to come along?"

"That's very generous, but no. You guys should enjoy a second honeymoon. It's almost your first anniversary," Kelsey replied.

"Can you believe I've managed to stay married to Ryan Perkins for a whole year?" Jessica said, and Kelsey laughed.

"I'm still getting over the fact that you said yes to a date to Ryan," Kelsey admitted.

Jessica giggled. "Yeah, me too," Jess admitted.

"So will you see Kim when you're there?"

"I'd say I hope not, but I know we will," Jessica said. "We aren't staying with her this time, though."

"Is Ryan trying to get you into the baby-making spirit?" Kelsey asked, and Jess burst out laughing.

"You had the same thought as me! I swear we're sisters. I totally think that Ryan's hoping that I'll see Kim with her baby and that will inspire me to do whatever he thinks I'm not doing."

"You need to buy Ryan a book on how babies are made," Kelsey said, with some seriousness.

"He just can't believe it's taken this long. He's so silly."

"It's been four months," Kelsey said. Jess and Ryan hadn't started trying for children until after the bar.

"Four months and eight days, give or take a couple, according to the human calendar that is my husband," Jess replied.

"Oh, Jess," Kelsey said sympathetically.

"I tossed out all of the pregnancy sticks in the house," Jessica said. "Ryan's been running after me every time I walk near the bathroom, and suggesting I test."

"He hasn't," Kelsey said.

"I'm completely serious," Jessica said. "Honestly, if he'd just calm down, it would probably happen for us."

"He needs to give it some time."

"Ryan is not known for his patience."

"True," Kelsey agreed.

"Anyway," Jessica said. "What do you want from L.A.?"

"Kelsey?" Leo asked on Friday.

"Yes?" Kelsey said looking up from her box. The students had been gathering their things to go.

"We're going out for drinks. Do you want to come along? Sam's meeting us there."

Kelsey thought for a moment. She didn't have to be up early.

"Sure, I'll go," she said.

"You might want to change," Rhian said, coming over. Kelsey glanced down. She was wearing a black sheath and her pearls today.

"I think you're right," Kelsey agreed.

Kelsey met the students in the lobby of the Sheraton fifteen minutes later. She had changed into a pair of jeans and a fitted navy t-shirt. The students clapped and Kelsey laughed.

"I didn't know you owned jeans," Jordan commented. Kelsey shrugged.

"Let's go," Leo said, and the group headed out.

On the walk there was a spirited discussion about which of Phoenix's bars the group would end up at. Finally, the students agreed on one, and Leo messaged Sam with their choice. He hadn't made it to the bar by the time they arrived, so the group headed in without him.

The party was in full swing when they entered. Kelsey looked around at the huge bar.

"There are two dance floors, each with a different DJ," Rhian told Kelsey over the noise.

"What do you want to drink, Kelsey?" Leo asked her.

"Ginger ale," Kelsey replied.

"Seriously?" Leo said doubtfully.

"I don't drink," Kelsey said unconcernedly.

"Ginger ale it is," Leo replied, and he wandered off.

"Let's go dance," Jordan said to Kelsey and Paloma, and the next thing Kelsey knew, she was being pulled to the dance floor. Leo came up a few minutes later, holding several drinks. Each of the girls took theirs.

"How much do I owe you?" Kelsey asked.

"We'll settle up later," Leo replied, drinking. "Enjoy."

Kelsey took a sip of her drink, and continued to dance.

A while later, the group headed up to the open air rooftop bar, where, as Rhian had said, there was a second DJ. To her surprise, and delight, the DJ was playing one of her favorite Hydronic songs. The Seattle band was coming out with a new album next spring, and Kelsey and Jess had already discussed getting tickets for the concert that the band was sure to have to support the album.

Kelsey's hair was loose and swinging in the desert air as she danced. Kelsey really liked this particular DJ's music and she stayed on the dance floor with Paloma, who seemed to like dancing as well.

"Ms. North can dance," Samuel said, as he joined them, drink in hand.

"Ms. North can do a lot of things," Kelsey corrected. Samuel laughed.

Kelsey and the group danced, drank, ate, and finally ended up sitting together in the night air talking, as the party continued.

"I wouldn't have pegged you as a club rat," Samuel said, drinking from a bottle.

Kelsey giggled. "Yeah, I'm not really."

"You're a in-bed-by-ten girl?" Samuel teased.

"Maybe twelve," Kelsey replied.

"I'm shocked," Samuel replied.

"I'm at work until ten," Kelsey said.

"That I believe," Samuel said. "What do you do for fun?"

Kelsey felt her heart jolt as she thought of Tyler.

"Lots of things," Kelsey replied noncommittally.

"Name one," Samuel said.

"I like to go dancing," Kelsey replied. *Thanks to Tyler*, she thought, but didn't say.

"I guessed that. We had to drag you off the floor. Are you sure you aren't a club rat?"

"I'm sure," Kelsey replied. She glanced at her cup, which was empty.

"Want some?" Samuel said, offering her his drink.

"No, thanks," Kelsey said.

"What are you drinking? I'll get you another."

"Ginger ale, but that's OK. I'll get more later."

"You don't drink?" Samuel said in surprise.

"No," Kelsey said.

"Such a good girl," Samuel commented. Kelsey glanced at him.

Although they were hanging out casually, she was still Samuel's boss, and she was surprised by the comment. Perhaps he had had more to drink than she thought.

"Just because I don't drink doesn't mean I'm a goody-two-shoes," Kelsey retorted.

"It doesn't?"

"No," Kelsey commented.

"OK. So what's the most risky thing you've done in Arizona?"

"Sam, I'm working. I don't have time for risky things," Kelsey replied.

"Fine. In the past year," Samuel said, opening up the question.

Kelsey thought for a moment. After her wild teenage years, Kelsey had created a life of stability, not one of insecurity, and she liked it. Her days of placing herself in danger for a momentary rush were over.

"I'm a goody-two-shoes," Kelsey concluded.

Samuel laughed. "I knew it."

"I'm a lawyer. Lawyers don't like risk."

Samuel was thoughtful. "I suppose that's true." He leaned back on the sofa they were sitting on and looked at her. "I bet you're more exciting than you let on, though."

"Why?" Kelsey said.

"Straight-laced lawyers don't have platinum blonde hair," Samuel said, looking at Kelsey's face.

"This one does."

"I'm thinking there's more to you than meets the eye," Samuel concluded, and he took another drink.

A few hours later, Kelsey lay in her bed and looked at the ends of her hair. Samuel's comments made her wonder what signals she was sending out to the legal community. She loved the color, but being a natural blonde, Kelsey was well aware of the negative stereotypes that came with the hair color. In high school, she had become a virtual encyclopedia of blonde jokes, having heard them all. Perhaps it was time for a new look.

As for the rest of Samuel's comments, Kelsey decided to ignore them. She wasn't moving to Arizona, Samuel wasn't her type, and most importantly, she wasn't interested in anyone but Tyler.

Roger visited the group on Saturday afternoon. Kelsey smiled when she saw him. He was wearing kelly-green pants embroidered with tiny bright pink flamingos, and he had a taxi-yellow sweater thrown over his shoulders. Clearly, from his outfit, he was heading to play golf after his visit.

"How's it going?" he asked her. They had walked outside of the boardroom, so as to be out of the earshot of the students.

"Good," Kelsey said.

"Everyone hanging in? Any problems?"

"None," Kelsey said. "Everyone is working hard, and it's a really good group."

"Fantastic. Bill mentioned that he was a little concerned about Jake."

"Jake's fine," Kelsey said.

"Great. Well, if you have things under control, I'll go enjoy my Saturday," Roger said.

"Have fun playing golf," Kelsey said.

"How did you know I was playing golf?" Roger asked, puzzled.

"You aren't working during the break, are you?" Kelsey asked Tyler during their normal phone call.

"I'm going to New York," Tyler replied.

"To see Chris?" Kelsey asked in surprise.

"To see Liz," Tyler corrected.

"Nice," Kelsey said. She knew that Tyler was close to his father's ex-girlfriend, but she had never known Tyler to visit her.

"Are you going home?" he asked.

"I hope so."

"You've got to be done by then, right?" Tyler asked.

"We'll be done soon," Kelsey replied. Although they still hadn't found what they were looking for, they had almost run out of boxes. With less than ten to go, Kelsey had no doubt she'd be back in her childhood bed on Christmas Eve.

"Never again," Tyler said, without explanation. "It's late. Are you in your room?" he asked.

"I am."

"I'll let you go to bed. Talk to you tomorrow?"

"Of course."

"Good night, Kelsey," Tyler said.

"Good night," Kelsey said, and they disconnected.

"Kelsey!" one of the work study students said at 8 p.m. on Tuesday night. Kelsey walked over, wiping her fingers as she did. They had ordered pizza again, and Samuel had brought a giant jar of candy canes, one of which had made Kelsey's fingers sticky.

"Is this what we're looking for?" the student, Rhian, asked. Kelsey carefully picked up the memo. She looked over it quickly. All of the eyes of the students were on her as she stood there. Kelsey turned the page, then a wide grin spread over her face.

"This is it," Kelsey said happily.

A few hours later, Kelsey got off the phone with Bill. She had scanned and sent the memo, which outlined the release strategy for the opposing side's product, along several other critical documents she and the students had found in the same box. Kelsey had left a message for Jake, and one for Tyler, who wasn't picking up his phone.

Bill had asked Kelsey to stay and finish the last two boxes, in case there were any other useful documents, arrange with Roger Morang to have everything put into storage, and most importantly, send Jake home.

The next day, Jake gave Kelsey a hug as he dropped by the boardroom on his way to the airport.

"Are you sure you're OK with staying by yourself?" he asked.

"I'll go home tomorrow," Kelsey said. "Say hi to Sara."

"I will," Jake said. "Have a good holiday."

"You too. Will I see you in the new year?" Kelsey teased.

"Unless I come to my senses and quit," Jake replied.

Kelsey sat at the table as Samuel packed up the last box at 4:55 p.m. that evening.

"So you're heading home tomorrow?" he asked. They were the only two in the room, as Kelsey had said goodbye to the students earlier in the afternoon.

"I am."

"I'm sorry we didn't get to hang out together," Samuel said.

"We had a lot of work to do," Kelsey replied.

"Well, if you're ever back in Phoenix, you should look me up," Samuel said.

Kelsey nodded. She wasn't sure if she would be back any time soon, unless Bill sent her again.

"It was nice working with you," Kelsey said. "If you need a recommendation let me know, and I'd be happy to write one."

Samuel surveyed Kelsey and sighed gently. He picked up his backpack.

"You're always professional, Ms. North," he commented. "Have a good holiday."

"Bye, Samuel," Kelsey said and Samuel left.

Kelsey stood and lifted the box off the large table. She hadn't been oblivious to Samuel's attraction to her over the past few weeks, but Kelsey had a project to run.

And of course, her heart was already taken.

Kelsey hung out at the pool for one final time the next morning. The sun shone in her face, and she enjoyed what she expected were her last warm rays of sunshine for a while. She knew that Seattle was in the midst of the cool, rainy winter, and she would be flying back today.

She had debated whether to go back to work or go straight to Port Townsend, but Bill Simon had ordered Kelsey not to come back to work until January 2nd. She had missed a month of Sundays, so Kelsey appreciated the offer and decided to take Bill up on it. The fact that Ryan and Jess were going to L.A. and that Tyler was leaving Seattle tomorrow night to visit Liz helped with the decision as well.

Kelsey was a little concerned about spending two weeks at home, but she had made it through a week in the summer with only the usual amount of drama, and the fact that Grandma Rose was coming for a week-long visit made Port Townsend more appealing.

She turned on the chaise lounge and looked up at the blue sky. Arizona had been good for her. The Landau project had kept her busy, and it was a great success for the client, which made Kelsey look good too. She had been too swamped to worry about Tyler, which was good, because she knew as soon as they got back, she would be concerned again.

Tyler had been working non-stop ever since she had left, but she still had no idea what on. Millie had told Kelsey that Marie had expressed their concern over Tyler to Bill, but Bill had assured the receptionists that Tyler's project would be over in the spring. This was no comfort to Kelsey, as spring was months away.

Kelsey ran her hand through her hair, which was now a soft summer blonde, and very close to her normal hair color again. She had gone to the salon last night after she had finished work, and after she had turned the keys of the empty boardroom back over to the hotel manager. She had enjoyed her time as a platinum blonde bombshell, but it was time for a change, and she was happy with her new look. Of course she needed to avoid the pool today — however, Kelsey felt that the tradeoff was worth it.

Kelsey closed her eyes and felt the warmth of the sun on her face. She only had a few hours until her flight, and it was finally time for her to relax.

Kelsey got off the plane at Sea-Tac, and walked through the terminal wheeling her suitcase behind her, with sunglasses in her hair. She felt very sophisticated and more than a little grown-up. She was a lawyer, returning from her first business trip, and she had done what she had been asked to do. Kelsey couldn't help but feel proud.

She walked out to the pick-up zone outside of baggage claim, and waved when she saw her driver. Jasmine waved back. Kelsey walked over, and Jasmine popped open the trunk of her car. Kelsey put her bag inside, closed it, and got into the passenger seat.

Jasmine leaned over for a hug.

"Again with the hair," Jasmine said, as Kelsey put on her seat belt. "How many times have you changed the color this year?"

Kelsey giggled.

"I'm going to take away your salon card," Jasmine commented as they pulled away from the curb.

"I needed a new look," Kelsey commented.

"You just had a new look," Jasmine said.

"Jazz, you change your hair every week. Give me a break," Kelsey replied. "How's everyone?"

"Great," Jasmine said, looking over her shoulder as she changed lanes. "We're excited that you're coming back home. We weren't sure you would return."

"Ha, ha," Kelsey said, looking out on the gray Seattle day. Her sexy sunglasses wouldn't be needed for a while.

"So what do you want to do over the holidays?" Jasmine asked as they drove out of the airport.

Kelsey shrugged. "The usual," she said.

"Are you going to work in the store?" Jasmine asked.

"Probably. It's not like I have anything else to do," Kelsey said.

"You aren't going to do any work over the break?" Jasmine said.

"The office is closed and we're all on call, but Seattle's legal community pretty much shuts down for Christmas," Kelsey said.

Of course the courts were open this week, but Kelsey knew that there was an unspoken gentleman's agreement between many of the law firms that Simon and Associates worked against not to file motions until the new year. No one wanted to have a ruined holiday.

"Lucky you," Jasmine said, as she merged on I-5 South. Kelsey knew that Jasmine would take the southern route to Port Townsend, as it would cut a ferry ride and almost an hour off the trip, even though it was an extra thirty miles to drive.

"Is Papa making you work this week?" Kelsey asked.

"Of course," Jasmine said. Kelsey wasn't surprised. "But we'll have fun anyway."

"Is Jace still at home?" Kelsey asked.

"He is," Jasmine said happily.

Kelsey was less enthusiastic. "Did he finish his thesis?" she asked.

"No, and Papa's pretty unhappy about that," Jasmine said.

"I bet he is," Kelsey said. Papa Jefferson hadn't been particularly happy with Jace's course of study, so she knew that he wouldn't be pleased that Jace wasn't on track to graduate.

"Jace said that it's more complex than he expected, but that it's going to be really good once he's done," Jasmine said. "I'm looking forward to reading it."

Kelsey didn't doubt this. Jasmine adored her annoying older brother. It was one of the many mysteries of life.

"What do you want to do over the holiday?" Kelsey asked.

"Mama wants us all to have Christmas Eve dinner, and she asked Morgan to come," Jasmine said.

Kelsey looked at Jasmine. "They're talking again?" Kelsey asked.

"A little," Jasmine replied.

Kelsey was pleased to hear it. "Good," she said. "When was the last time you saw Morgan?"

"We had lunch at Ben's last week," Jasmine said. Kelsey was happy to hear this as well. She, Jasmine, and Morgan had always been close, but Morgan's relationship with Bob — and to a lesser extent, Kelsey's relationship with Tyler — had put a bump in the girls' friendship. Kelsey wanted to believe that things were improving. She knew she'd find out over the next two weeks.

Jasmine took I-5 past Fife and turned onto Route 16. Kelsey thought of her mother's parents as they drove through Gig Harbor, but she knew she wouldn't be seeing them soon. For this she was grateful. Unlike her own mother, who was slowly beginning to see the error of her ways, Kelsey suspected that her maternal grandparents still thought of her as the rebellious teenager she had been before. She had no desire to spend the energy trying to change their minds.

They slowly weaved their way up the Olympic Peninsula and chatted about mutual friends in Port Townsend and potential activities for Kelsey's vacation. Kelsey knew that she wouldn't see Jasmine as much as she would see Morgan, for the simple reason that Jasmine was married.

But as they drove toward their hometown, Kelsey was hopeful that maybe the short time they would spend together would begin to rebuild the affection the girls had once shared.

Jasmine drove Kelsey back to the North house. As soon as she drove up, the front door of the house opened, and Kelsey's father walked out. Kelsey jumped out of the car and ran into her beloved father's arms.

"Hey, Kels," Dan North said happily, giving her a warm hug. "Jasmine, don't you touch that bag," he called. Kelsey released him, and he walked over to the trunk of Jasmine's car.

"I was going to help," Jasmine pouted, as Dan North pulled Kelsey's bag out of the trunk.

"Jasmine, that bag is almost as big as you," Dan North chided the petite Jasmine.

"Thank you for helping, Dan," Jasmine said.

"You're welcome. Are you coming in?" he asked, as Kelsey walked back over to the car.

Jasmine shook her head, and her long black hair brushed her shoulders. "I have to go make dinner." she replied.

"Thanks for picking me up," Kelsey said.

Jasmine gave Kelsey a hug. "Any time. See you Saturday?"

"Of course," Kelsey replied.

"Bye, Dan," Jasmine said, giving him a wave as she headed back to her car.

"Goodbye, Jasmine. Give my regards to your parents," Dan North said. Kelsey waved as Jasmine drove off, then she followed her father into the house.

"What's in this?" Dan North said, pulling the bag into a corner of the living room.

"Jess and Ryan came for a visit and bought out every boutique in Phoenix," Kelsey replied, looking around her childhood home.

"I see. You should invite them back to Port Townsend. There's a few merchants who could use their largess."

"Is the store doing OK?" Kelsey asked in concern.

"Our store is doing great," Dan North said with confidence.

"OK," Kelsey said doubtfully.

Her father smiled at her look. "Kelsey Anne, sales have gone up 15% this year. So stop worrying."

"Really?" Kelsey said in surprise.

"Everyone's choosing to staycation around here. They need camping and outdoor equipment. But they aren't buying a lot of clothes. We're fine, but I'm a little concerned about some of our neighbors. That's all."

"If you say so," Kelsey said, slightly relieved. Ever since Lisa Olsen's attack, Kelsey always felt anxious about her parents' livelihood, despite the fact that thanks to Tyler, she owned the building their store was located in and her parents owned their home free and clear. Kelsey knew her feelings were irrational, but she also knew that she hadn't completely dealt with the stresses of the past year.

"So after I drag this upstairs for you, what do you want to do?" her father asked gesturing to the bag.

Kelsey shrugged. "I could make dinner," she said.

"Aren't you supposed to be on vacation?" her father asked in amusement.

"I guess," Kelsey said.

"I don't want you going into the store for at least a week," Dan North said sharply. "You need some downtime."

Kelsey nodded. She supposed that was true. Despite her off-hours hanging out by the Sheraton pool, she had been working a lot over the past month.

Her father picked up the bag and began maneuvering it across the living room and up the stairs. Kelsey followed him.

"Rose is coming on Tuesday," he said.

Kelsey couldn't help but smile. She adored her grandmother. "Do you want me to pick her up?"

"You aren't going to relax this vacation, are you?" Dan North said, as he wheeled the bag to Kelsey's bedroom.

"Dad, it's not a big deal to drive to Port Angeles. Anyway, it's not like I have anything else to do."

"You could sit on the sofa. Watch TV. Read."

"I'm sure I'll do plenty of that as well. Morgan and Jasmine are both working while I'm here," Kelsey commented. In fact, she wouldn't see Morgan before Monday, because she had gone to Seattle for a meeting planners conference.

Kelsey also knew, although she knew that Ryan didn't, that Morgan would spend the rest of her weekend in Medina. This weekend was the Tactec holiday party, and Morgan Hill would be Bob Perkins's date this year. Ryan would find out at the event.

Dan North wheeled Kelsey's bag into her room, and Kelsey looked around in amusement. One of her tasks this weekend would be to clear out her room. It still looked the way it had when she had been in high school.

"Your mom will be home soon, and we can head out and get dinner," her father said.

"That would be great," Kelsey said.

"There's probably something in the fridge if you're hungry."

"I had a snack on the plane, I'm fine," Kelsey replied.

Her father gave her hair a kiss. "Welcome home, Kelsey," he said, and he left.

Five hours later, Kelsey was standing on her bed, pulling down a poster. She had gone to dinner with her parents, which to her relief had been uneventful. Her mother had been in a good mood, perhaps because there were still a few days until Grandma Rose arrived. They had returned home, watched a little TV, then Kelsey had returned to her room to reorganize it.

She was almost done, and Kelsey wasn't surprised that it had happened so quickly. Unlike a lot of people, Kelsey didn't look back on her teenage years as a happy time, one where the world was an exciting unknown, ready to be conquered. Instead, Kelsey's youth was a time of wild excess, then unpleasant soul-searching. She had been grateful to leave her teenage years behind, and clearing her room was one of the final steps.

As she stuffed the old poster into a garbage bag, Kelsey wondered why it had taken so long for her to do this. She had wanted to for many years, but every time she had been in Port Townsend, she had put the task off.

Perhaps she needed to feel like an adult to finally say goodbye to her childhood.

Her dresser was completely empty, save for Tyler's jewelry box, and the two pairs of diamond earrings that sat inside. Kelsey thought that this year she would finally bring these pieces back to Seattle. She had a safe deposit box, so she wouldn't have to worry about the earrings' safety, and despite the hundred thousand dollars of Tyler's money that was sitting inside, there would still be plenty of room.

Kelsey placed a third stuffed bear into the soft chair that sat in the corner of her room. She had sat in that chair for days throughout her childhood, thinking about her life — past, present, and future. It was there that she had plotted new trouble to get into with Eric, pondered the ordeals that she had got herself into, and planned for her new, brighter future.

The future she was living now.

Kelsey loved her new life as a lawyer, despite the long hours and the missed weekends. She had always dreamed of living in the city, and of living her own life, and now she did. She didn't have to ask permission, request money, or borrow a car. She could just make a decision and go.

Of course, Kelsey couldn't have everything she wanted, whenever she wanted to have it. This was one thing that she had learned as she had become an adult, and she had finally begun to accept it.

And that of course, was where her relationship with Tyler came in.

On Friday, Kelsey heeded her father's advice and didn't go down to the store. Instead, she took a bike out of the shed, and rode to Fort Worden. Kelsey hadn't been there in a long time, even though it was minutes from her home. She rode into the park, and spent three hours riding past the historic buildings, walking on the cold beaches, and letting the winds blow through her hair.

She returned home in the afternoon, refreshed from a morning of being in her beloved wilderness. She had loved Arizona, but she had missed the distinctive features of the Pacific Northwest while she had been there.

The Olympic Peninsula had a bit of an edge. Beaches were just as likely to be sharp rock as sandy shore, evergreen trees towered over people reminding one that nature was still in charge, and whether the cold rain arrived could make all of the difference between a pleasant day and a miserable one.

Kelsey's cheeks felt raw from the cold as she stood in the family kitchen and made a sandwich. For years, Kelsey had always had mixed emotions when she returned to Port Townsend. Her past haunted her, because she feared that the same impulses that had ruined her life once, remained ready to arise and ruin it again. But today, on this visit, Kelsey felt a confidence that had eluded her in the past. For the first time, she was in control, not of her situation, but of herself.

Kelsey's newfound emotional control was tested when her mother arrived home a few hours later. Kelly North's mood was upbeat, and Kelsey knew from vast experience that that didn't always work in her favor. It usually meant that her mother had a brilliant idea. For Kelsey.

Kelsey found out quickly what Kelly North had in mind for her, once they were sitting for dinner. Kelsey had been stirring her hot chili quietly, when her mother fixed her with a look.

"Brent Smith has moved to Seattle."

Brent Smith? Kelsey thought for a moment. She had lived in Port Townsend all of her life, and knew something about most families in the area, but the name didn't ring a bell at first. Then she remembered.

The captain of her high school football team.

Her father coughed, and Kelsey suspected that he was covering up a laugh. Kelly North glared at him, but turned to Kelsey with a smile.

"Brent has been working in California, but his company transferred him up to Seattle last month."

"That's great," Kelsey said unenthusiastically.

"He told his mother that he remembers you, and that he'd love to get together when you get back."

"I bet," Kelsey replied cooly.

"And what does that mean, Kelsey Anne?" Kelly North said in irritation.

Kelsey sighed softly. She wasn't sure what to say to her mother. Kelsey had spent more than a few moments of her high school career fending off guys who assumed that she was easy because of her relationship with Eric Johns. It was why she hadn't done a lot of dating in high school. In fact, she had gone to prom with Ben for the simple reason that she had no desire to deal with most of the rest of the boys in her high school class. And at the top of the list of the guys that Kelsey had no desire to deal with was Brent Smith.

"It means that Brent and I weren't really friends in high school," Kelsey said.

"Well, Brent understands that you had some issues then, but he knows that you're over them," her mother replied.

Kelsey's mouth dropped open, and her father turned to his wife in surprise.

"Are you kidding me?" Kelsey snapped. "I had issues? You should talk to the people who hung out with Brent."

"Kelly, Kelsey's an adult now, and a successful lawyer," Dan North began, but his wife cut him off.

"Dan, just because you're deluding yourself that Tyler Olsen is going to turn Kelsey into Cinderella, doesn't mean that Kelsey shouldn't be dating other people."

Dan North frowned. "I think that Kelsey's relationship with Tyler is her business," he commented.

"Oh, come on Dan. You've talked to him every few weeks for months. I'm sure he's still pretending that he's going to marry Kelsey so he doesn't lose his friendship with you. Once Kelsey gets married, he's off the hook and he can marry the socialite that his mother expects him to."

Kelsey and her father looked at each other, then at Kelly North, who was frowning. Kelsey knew that Dan North was trying to figure out how to gracefully get out of this conversation, just like she was. Kelsey decided to try first.

"Mom, I'm really too busy to date anyone right now," Kelsey said.

Kelly North looked aghast.

"You aren't going on dates?" she said. Kelsey realized that she had misspoken. More than anything, Kelly North wanted Kelsey to be married. She believed that it would settle her only daughter down.

"I've been on a couple," Kelsey lied.

"See, Kelsey doesn't need our help in finding a husband," her father said soothingly. "And maybe Brent Smith isn't the kind of boy Kelsey is interested in."

"And Tyler Olsen is?" Kelly North said angrily.

"I didn't say that," Dan North replied. "But," he added, taking Kelsey by surprise, "the fact is that they did go out for quite a while, so perhaps he is."

"Daniel North," Kelsey's mother said sharply, "How can you continue to get Kelsey's hopes up on Tyler Olsen?"

"I'm not."

"Of course you are. What do you think Kelsey thinks right now, knowing that Tyler's in touch with you?"

"Kelly, Kelsey works in the same office as Tyler. She knows what Tyler's thinking," Dan North said in irritation.

Suddenly, the table was totally, utterly silent. Kelly North looked at her husband with wide eyes, and Kelsey sat completely still. And at that moment, she and her father realized that he had said exactly the wrong thing to his wife of over two decades.

"Tyler Olsen works in the same office as Kelsey?" Kelly North said, standing and raising her voice. She turned to Kelsey in outrage. "Tyler Olsen works with you?"

Kelsey looked helplessly at her father, who was looking at his dinner in obvious discomfort.

"Yes," Kelsey said, in almost a whisper.

Kelly North went pale. Then she left the room.

"Kelsey, I'm sorry," Dan North said, looking at her.

She reached out a hand, and patted his. "Actually, Dad, I'm sorry for you," Kelsey said honestly.

Later that evening, Kelsey lay back on her bed, headphones on, in a vain attempt to drown out her mother's shouting. Kelsey had heard the beginning of the argument, where Kelly North accused her husband of hiding information from her, and Dan North insisted that it had been merely an oversight. But the argument had moved from Kelly North's anger to a debate over whether Tyler Olsen would ever be suitable for Kelsey. And Kelsey wasn't interested in hearing it. She knew, as did her father, that despite Kelly North's strong views, that Kelsey would not grant her mother a vote.

Kelsey had heard enough of the argument to know that although Kelly North didn't fault Tyler for the break-up, she was horrified that Dan North would consider letting Kelsey marry into a family that had done so much damage to Kelsey, and to the North family. Dan North insisted that Tyler wouldn't ask Kelsey to marry him until things had been cleared up with Lisa Olsen, and that Kelly North didn't need to worry. However, Kelsey's mother was not appeased, so the argument went on.

Things finally quieted down after a while, and Kelsey peeked carefully out of her bedroom door. She wandered downstairs, and hearing nothing but the television, Kelsey walked to the basement. Her father sat in front of the television, a hockey game on, the remote and a plate of cookies next to him. Kelsey sat on the sofa and took a cookie.

"You're alive," she commented.

"Barely," Dan North replied with a smile.

"Is she OK?" Kelsey asked.

"I don't think she's going to divorce me."

"Is that a plus?" Kelsey teased.

"I'd like to think so," her father said, giving Kelsey a look.

"I'm sorry to get between you and Mom," she said seriously.

"It's not your fault," Kelsey's father said, breaking a cookie in half thoughtfully.

"It is, though. If Mom thought I had some sense, she wouldn't always be trying to run my life. And you wouldn't always be fighting against that."

"Kelsey, this isn't about you. Your mother is concerned about what marrying into the Olsen family would be like for you, and I don't blame her. Rose is concerned about the same thing."

"And you?" Kelsey asked.

"I'm trying to reserve judgment."

"Because Tyler wants you to," Kelsey said softly.

"Because I believe Tyler when he says that he loves you," Dan North corrected.

Kelsey sighed. "It doesn't matter. Tyler hasn't asked me to marry him."

"That's true," Dan conceded. "And perhaps he won't. But your mother and grandmother have every right to worry about what it means for you if you restart a romantic relationship with him."

Kelsey nodded. That was true. Lisa Olsen's wrath had affected them too.

"Kelsey, your mother loves you very much, and she only wants the best for you. She's not sure that Tyler is it."

"But you do?"

"Again, trying to reserve judgment," Dan North hedged.

"You should have been a lawyer," Kelsey said, finally taking a bite of her cookie.

"I think one in this house is enough," her father replied.

Things were quiet at breakfast the next morning, but to Kelsey's surprise they weren't particularly tense. She supposed her parents had made up. Her father left to check on her building before opening the store, and Kelsey and her mother sat at the table, drinking coffee and finishing breakfast.

"Do you still love him?"

Kelsey looked at her mother. "Yes," she replied.

Her mother sighed. "I know you won't listen if I give you my opinion," she said.

"Probably not," Kelsey admitted.

"OK," Kelly North said. She drained her cup, stood up, and left the room.

Jasmine drove up at 11 a.m. and beeped the horn. Kelsey put her Kindle on the living room table, grabbed her navy fleece jacket, and headed outside.

"How's it going?" Jasmine asked as Kelsey got into the car and strapped herself in.

"It's going," Kelsey said noncommittally as Jasmine drove off.

Jasmine laughed. "You hate coming home, don't you?"

"My mother is always a pain," Kelsey replied.

"I don't understand why you don't get along with Kelly. I think she's great."

"That's because you know how to behave. She likes people who follow the rules."

"I suppose you have a point," Jasmine agreed.

"So she wanted to set me up with Brent Smith," Kelsey said.

"I thought he was in Silicon Valley."

"I guess he's back," Kelsey said with a shrug. "He lives in Seattle now."

"So what did you say?"

"I said no. He's a jerk," Kelsey replied.

"Is he? I don't remember."

"That's because you get along with everyone."

"No, I don't," Jasmine said.

"You did in high school," Kelsey replied.

"There weren't that many people to get along with," Jasmine replied.

"A hundred. That's enough people to find a few not to like."

"You knew you were leaving. I've got to live with the people we went to school with."

"I suppose," Kelsey said. "Where are we going?"

"Silverdale. I thought I'd bring my own car this time."

Kelsey laughed. The last time they had gone to Silverdale together, Dylan had abandoned them, and they had to get a ride with Tyler's chauffeur.

"What are you looking for?" Kelsey asked.

"I need a warmer sweater," Jasmine said.

"You should just come to Seattle and go shopping," Kelsey said.

"I'm not Morgan."

"What do you mean?" Kelsey asked.

"You know she's in Seattle with her boyfriend now."

"I know," Kelsey said. She wondered where Jasmine was going with this.

"Every time she comes back, she has new clothes," Jasmine shrugged.

Kelsey wasn't surprised. "Every time I see Jess, I have new clothes too," Kelsey said.

"I guess," Jasmine conceded, and she dropped the subject.

Kelsey followed Jasmine around the mall for the rest of the afternoon. There wasn't anything that Kelsey needed, and she had already bought her Christmas gifts for everyone. Jasmine, on the other hand, bought a lot. They settled into a restaurant near the end of her shopping spree, to fuel up for the ride home.

"I'm impressed," Kelsey commented, as Jasmine folded and replaced a sweater in one of her bags.

"I needed a few things," Jasmine replied. "I don't have billionaires to buy things for me."

Kelsey sat silently. In addition to Jess, of course, Tyler still bought Kelsey things too.

"Do you think that's why she's staying with him?" Jasmine asked. Kelsey knew she was talking about Morgan. She hesitated. Although all of the girls spoke freely about each other, Kelsey wasn't sure she wanted to start this particular conversation.

"I think Morgan loves him," Kelsey said. Of course, even Kelsey had had her doubts, but Morgan said that she loved Bob, and that was enough for Kelsey.

"Hmm," Jasmine replied, and fell silent.

Kelsey was happy to arrive back at home on Saturday evening. Her father had taken her mother out for dinner, as a sort of apology for not telling her about Tyler, and Kelsey was on her own. Ben had been promising to visit for three days running, but the cafe was taking so much of his free time. Kelsey figured that she would have lunch there at some point during the holidays.

Tyler had sent her a brief message before he boarded his plane yesterday, and made a point of telling her that he would be buying a new phone in New York, so she should expect to see a different number in the next few days. Kelsey had experienced this before with Tyler, although usually Jeffrey was the one to share the new number with Kelsey. She supposed that Jeffrey hadn't accompanied Tyler to New York, so he would be taking care of it himself.

On Sunday morning, things were back to normal with her parents. Her father prepared breakfast before heading down to the store, and Kelsey's mom made a point of giving him a warm kiss as he was about to walk out the door.

Kelsey went for a long run, passing by her former high school, which was only a few blocks away. Kelsey was reminded of Dylan, and his hesitation to return to Darrow, when she ran past. Memories were not always kind.

Kelsey sat at the kitchen table reading as the winter sun began to fade on Sunday afternoon. She was feeling relaxed after months of stress. To her surprise though, she was becoming bored. Kelsey had cleaned her room, seen Jasmine, gone shopping, cooked, baked, gone biking and for walks, and she felt like she was running out of things to do. Although it certainly wasn't an excuse, Kelsey remembered why she had created so much drama when she had lived here before.

More than anything though, Kelsey knew the major difference between this and other trips home over the past few years.

Tyler.

Kelsey was grateful that she knew he was safe, and spending time with Liz, and that Kelsey didn't need to worry. But she missed him so much. When she was in Arizona, it was easy to bury herself in work, but here, there was nothing to do. So she longed for him.

Of course, she longed for him when he was working down the hall, when she was sitting across from him eating lunch, or generally every other moment of her day.

Kelsey had spent so much time with him here, Port Townsend no longer felt like home without him. Although her mind didn't want to admit it, Kelsey knew what her heart felt.

Home had become where Tyler was.

"How was it?" Kelsey asked Morgan on Monday evening. She had just scrolled through a dozen pictures of Morgan and Bob from the Tactec holiday party. Morgan had worn a stunning black gown, and a diamond necklace which had been rented for the evening.

"Strange," Morgan replied, as she twisted her highlighted brown hair on her finger.

"Why?"

"Not because of Bob," Morgan explained. "Because of Tyler."

"Tyler was there?" Kelsey asked. She realized that she had assumed that he would skip the event to avoid Lisa, but she had never asked. Jess had sent her a message that Morgan had been at the party, but had said nothing more.

"No," Morgan said. Kelsey frowned in confusion. "He was supposed to be there."

Kelsey listened as Morgan explained.

"I guess Tyler had told the PR department that he would be attending. So there's a place setting for Tyler next to Lisa at the table, but it's empty. After the main course, Lisa gestured to a PR person, and tells her to find out where Tyler was."

Morgan continued. "So eventually, Tyler's assistant shows up wearing a suit, and he looks particularly unhappy to be there. He speaks to Lisa, who looks absolutely furious at whatever he's saying to her. She waves him away, and puts her CEO smile on her face, but that was it for the evening. You could tell that she was really upset."

"I wonder what happened?" Kelsey said. But then she realized. "Tyler's in New York," she blurted out. *Of course*, Kelsey thought to herself. *He sent me a message.* She explained to Morgan: "He left Friday night."

"If he left Friday night, he knew he wasn't flying back on Saturday,"

Morgan pointed out.

"But why would he tell Jeffrey he was attending?" Kelsey wondered, but as the words came out, she knew. *To upset Lisa.*

"You know better than I do," Morgan commented.

"Yeah, I guess I do," Kelsey said. "Did you hear Jeffrey say where Tyler was?"

Morgan shook her head. "Not that night. But Bob told me on Sunday that Tyler was with his father's ex-girlfriend, and that Tyler would stay there for Christmas. Bob said that he wasn't looking forward to going back to work today. That Lisa would go ballistic, because Tyler had missed Thanksgiving as well."

"I see," Kelsey said.

"Do you know what's going on between them? Tyler and Lisa? Bob said that they haven't talked in months."

"They're fighting," Kelsey said.

"Over you?" Morgan asked wisely.

"Partly," Kelsey said thoughtfully. "But I think something else is going on."

"Tyler hasn't told you?" Morgan asked.

Kelsey shook her head. "He hasn't," Kelsey said.

"I thought the two of you were OK."

"We are, but Tyler isn't talking about Lisa."

"Well, he sure managed to ruin Lisa's evening," Morgan said.

"Sadly, I have a feeling he might be pleased to find that out," Kelsey mused.

Kelsey put her grandmother's bag in the corner of the guest room on Tuesday as Grandma Rose sat on the edge of the bed she would be sleeping in during the next week.

"Is this OK?" Kelsey asked. "You can stay in my room if you want to. Both beds are still there."

Grandma Rose shook her head. "You don't need to hear my snoring," she said.

"You don't snore," Kelsey said.

"Your mother says I do," Grandma Rose replied. Kelly North and Grandma Rose had been forced to share a room at Kelsey's law school graduation and it hadn't gone well.

"Ignore her," Kelsey said bluntly.

"So you've been having fun with your mother?" Grandma Rose asked wisely.

"The same as always," Kelsey commented.

"Well, you only get one mother, so you have to make the most of life with her," Grandma noted.

"True," Kelsey said. "What do you want to do? Do you need a nap?"

"Kelsey Anne, I'm not a toddler."

Kelsey laughed. "I didn't mean it like that."

"I know. I'm just feeling my age these days," Grandma Rose said, standing up. "Come on, let's have some tea."

Late that night, Kelsey got a message from a new number. She knew it was Tyler.

Hi, Princess.

Kelsey looked at the time. It was midnight, which meant it was 3 a.m. in New York.

Hi. Why are you up?

Thinking of you.

Kelsey smiled.

How's New York? She typed.

Boring without you here. But Liz is fine. Tyler replied.

Where have you gone? Chelsea Market? The Highline? Kelsey asked, knowing that these were two of Tyler's favorite places.

Neither. Liz lives in the Village. I haven't been to Chelsea. Kelsey was surprised at first, but then she realized. Perhaps Tyler was concerned about running into his father if he went to his father's neighborhood. *We went to MOMA yesterday,* Tyler continued.

Did you see anything good? Kelsey asked, referring to the art.

No, because you're across the country, Tyler replied. *I miss you.*

I miss you too. But you should go to bed. Do you know what time it is?

I do, Tyler wrote.

Get some good sleep.

I will. I'll dream of you, Tyler replied. *I love you.*

Kelsey looked at the message in surprise. Tyler rarely wrote anything personal in his messages. Kelsey suspected it was because others had access to them. But Kelsey realized. Tyler had just bought a new phone.

I love you too, Tyler. Good night, Kelsey typed, happy to be able to express her feelings.

Good night, Princess. And with those words, Tyler signed off.

Kelsey stood next to her grandmother in the kitchen the next day, hands on her hips, blonde ponytail resting on her own shoulder.

"Pecans?" Kelsey asked.

"Do you think?" Grandma Rose asked thoughtfully.

"Walnuts are very traditional," Kelsey mused.

"I like them," Grandma commented. Kelsey liked them too. She knew why she was hesitating, though. Tyler didn't like walnuts. But of course, he wouldn't be eating any of the fudge they were preparing. He was still across the country, visiting Liz.

"Let's make it with pecans," Kelsey said definitively. "It will be a nice change."

"Sounds like a plan," Grandma Rose said, picking up the knife to chop the nuts. Suddenly the knife slipped out of her hand, and clattered onto the floor. Kelsey picked up the knife, and walked it over to the sink to wash it. As Kelsey handed it back, Grandma Rose shook her head. "I'm such a butterfingers lately," she said.

"It's not a big deal," Kelsey said, smiling at her grandmother. But as Kelsey looked at her, she noticed how much older Grandma Rose seemed this visit. She was aging, and Kelsey was feeling concerned.

"Is Grandma doing OK?" Kelsey asked her mother later. She would have preferred to ask her father, but since Grandma Rose was his mother, Kelsey didn't want to worry him.

"What do you mean?" Kelly North asked.

"Grandma seems a little more fragile," Kelsey said.

"Well, she's getting older, Kelsey."

"I know, but she dropped a few things when we were cooking today, and I was wondering what you thought."

Kelly leaned against the counter where she was standing. Kelsey's grandmother and father were in the basement watching television, and she and her mother were in the kitchen, putting away the dinner leftovers.

"I don't know, Kelsey," and she sighed, "I think Rose won't be able to live by herself too much longer."

"Grandma won't have to go to a retirement home, will she?" Kelsey asked. She couldn't picture her vibrant grandmother being happy surrounded by other seniors, and with nowhere to go.

"No, Kelsey. I think she'll have to move in here," Kelly North replied. Kelsey could hear the hesitation in her mother's voice. Kelly and Grandma Rose didn't get along, but Dan North was an only child, and he was responsible for his mother in her old age.

"Here?" Kelsey asked, stunned. She could only imagine what her grandmother would think of that plan.

117

"Maybe," Kelly North said. "Your father and I were discussing it last week. Port Angeles is a little far in an emergency."

Kelsey agreed. It was an hour from her parents' home to her grandmother's.

"Have you talked to her about it?" Kelsey asked.

Kelly shook her head. "We think that she can probably stay there for another year or so. She's pretty active with the senior center, and she's still going out every day on her own. Your father's going to make a point of visiting every few weeks and monitoring what's going on. But we probably need to get used to the idea."

"Grandma will need to get used to it as well."

"We'll talk to her later. You know how she's going to react."

"Yeah, I do," Kelsey replied. "Not well."

Kelsey was a bit more relaxed the next day as she and Grandma played Monopoly in the dining room the next day, knowing that her parents had a plan for Grandma's long-term care.

"How's Tyler?" Grandma asked out of the blue.

"OK," Kelsey replied. The last time they had played Monopoly, Tyler had played with them.

"I understand that things are OK in the office?" Grandma asked.

Kelsey knew how she knew. Her father and grandmother were close. "Much better," Kelsey said.

"Good. I was worried."

"It's OK."

"Are you still in love with him?" Grandma asked.

Kelsey felt her heart skip. She looked at her grandmother. "Yes," Kelsey admitted.

"Dan says he's still in love with you too."

"I know," Kelsey said as her grandmother rolled the dice.

"Are you sure things are OK?" Grandma asked wisely.

"Tyler says that he's working things out," Kelsey replied.

"But you don't think he is?" Grandma asked as she moved the little dog around to Park Place.

"I don't know what to think," Kelsey said.

"Do you trust him?" Grandma said.

"I do," Kelsey replied.

"I do too," Grandma replied. "Are you feeling impatient because things haven't worked out yet?"

"Yes," Kelsey said.

"I get the sense that Tyler's life is very complicated," Grandma said.

"I think that's a bit of an understatement," Kelsey replied.

That night, Kelsey lay in her room and looked at the ceiling. The last time she had been here — last summer — she had spent a week crying and worrying about Tyler. Now she wasn't crying, but once again Tyler was on her mind. He had messaged her this evening and wished her a good night. But she had so many questions, questions she couldn't ask. At least not now.

There was Tyler's non-attendance at the Tactec party. His mysterious weekends with Ryan, Zach, and Brandon, which had been going on for over two months. The strange conversation with Bill Simon, where they had been discussing a four-million-dollar project, that Tyler seemed to be the potential client for. And of course, the hundred thousand dollars sitting in Kelsey's bank.

Kelsey didn't doubt for a minute that it all made sense to Tyler, who despite everything, seemed like he had his life under control. Yet Kelsey had no idea what was going on at all.

When Kelsey woke up the next morning, she had made her resolution for the new year. When she returned to Seattle, and the moment that she saw Tyler Olsen, she would demand to have all of her questions answered.

Kelsey's patience with Tyler had run out.

On Saturday, Kelsey left Grandma at home to bake cookies, while she joined her parents at the store. It had been a while since she had been there, and before opening the store for customers, her father insisted on giving Kelsey a tour of the building. Her building.

Kelsey followed her father through the floors above the store, where offices were located. Kelsey walked along the warmly-lit corridor.

"Your mother and I did some painting a few weeks ago," Dan North said to Kelsey, pointing at the ceiling.

"Thanks for keeping it so nice," Kelsey said.

"It's my pleasure," her father said.

"When it goes back to Tyler, it would be good if it was in better shape than when I got it."

Her father smiled at her. "That makes sense," he commented.

"Why are you looking at me like that?" she asked.

"I'm not sure Tyler will be taking it back," her father commented.

"Dad, I can't keep this," Kelsey said.

"Have you talked to him about it?"

"No," Kelsey admitted. "You know I don't feel good about having this."

"I know," Dan said. "But I have a feeling that it's a lost cause."

As Kelsey worked in the store with her parents, and helped customers find their last-minute holiday gifts, she thought about her father's comment. She knew he was right — Tyler wouldn't take back the building. Or the thousands of dollars of rent it had generated since she received it. Probably, for Tyler, the amount of money wasn't worth talking about. It wouldn't be long before he would be in fully in charge of his two-billion-dollar inheritance, after all.

"Does this come in blue?" Kelsey's customer asked, knocking Kelsey out of her revery.

"I'll check," Kelsey said, with as much Christmas cheer as she could muster.

That evening, Kelsey sat on Morgan's sofa, and looked out over Water Street as Morgan made cocoa in her kitchen. Kelsey was wearing her pajamas. Morgan had invited Kelsey and Grandma to sleep over, but Grandma had declined, saying that she wanted the girls to have some quality time together.

Morgan walked over with two steaming mugs in her hands. She was wearing her pajamas as well, and her hair was in two pigtails. She handed a mug to Kelsey, and sat next to her on the sofa, folding her legs underneath herself. Kelsey blew on her mug, and the steam disappeared into the air as mini-marshmallows melted into the hot cocoa.

"So how is it at your house?" Morgan asked.

"Not bad," Kelsey commented. "Mom and Grandma are ignoring each other, instead of fighting. It's pretty quiet."

"It's a little sad that the best you can hope for is silence, babe," Morgan commented.

"I'll take what I can get," Kelsey said, taking a sip of the cocoa. It was delicious. "How are things at your dad's?"

Morgan shrugged. "The usual. Anna won't do anything."

Kelsey giggled. Morgan and her younger step-sister Anna were like oil and water, and always had been.

"How's your dad?" Kelsey asked.

"The same as always," Morgan commented. But Kelsey had known Morgan for a long time. There was something in her voice that sounded off.

"And?" Kelsey asked.

"I can never get anything past you," Morgan commented.

"Nope," Kelsey replied. "Tell me."

"He asked me when I was going to stop fooling around with Bob since he clearly wasn't going to marry me," Morgan commented.

Kelsey looked at Morgan in surprise. Morgan's father, as far as Kelsey knew, had never said anything about Bob to Morgan. So this was news.

"What did you say?" Kelsey asked.

Morgan took a sip of her cocoa.

"Well, the timing was interesting," Morgan mused. "It was a couple of days after you saw Bob with Fiona."

"Really?" Kelsey said. She knew that Morgan hadn't mentioned Fiona to anyone else, and of course Kelsey hadn't.

"Yeah. Anyway, I told my father that I would give it some thought."

"And he said?"

"He said that he was tired about hearing that his daughter was a harlot, and that he expected that as the oldest, I would set a better example for my sisters."

Kelsey looked at Morgan in disbelief. She knew that Walter Hill had never previously spoken to Morgan — or any of his daughters — in that way, severely, as a concerned father might. He had been content to let the girls raise themselves from childhood. Kelsey wondered why suddenly his perspective had changed so radically.

"It was weird. I honestly didn't think that he had an opinion," Morgan said. "He certainly took long enough to tell me."

"What are you going to do?" Kelsey asked, taking another sip of the warm cocoa. The marshmallows had melted and sweetened the drink.

"Think," Morgan said. "Bob invited me to the Tactec party to try to make up for you running into Fiona. But that's not what I want. I don't want to be Bob's part-time girlfriend. I want it all, and Bob knows it, and he's choosing to ignore me."

Morgan took a sip of cocoa, and added, "But, I don't have a plan B, so it's not like I can do that instead."

"Plan B could be breaking up with him," Kelsey replied.

Morgan shook her head. "I'm still not ready for that. I still have hope."

Kelsey understood that feeling. "Yeah, I get that," Kelsey said.

"So what should I do?" Morgan said.

"No idea," Kelsey said honestly.

"Me neither," Morgan said. "Tell me your life is better."

Kelsey thought for a moment. "Some days it doesn't feel like it, but it is."

"I'll live vicariously through you," Morgan said.

"Don't do that. You'll work all of the time," Kelsey said, half-seriously.

Morgan laughed. "Tyler's at war with Lisa, isn't he?" she asked.

"I don't know what Tyler's doing," Kelsey admitted.

"That's bothering you, isn't it?"

"Yeah, I don't do well with uncertainty. I always want to know what's going on."

"Have you asked him?"

Kelsey thought for a moment. "Not really," she replied.

"Are you going to?" Morgan asked.

"I think so."

"Do you think he's going to tell you?"

"I don't know. Maybe," Kelsey said.

"Bob seemed kind of concerned. He hasn't seen Tyler lately, and he said Ryan's not talking about him."

"What is Bob concerned about?" Kelsey asked. She didn't normally discuss Bob's conversations with Morgan, but since this involved Tyler, she felt like it was an exception.

Morgan seemed to agree, as she answered Kelsey's question. "Mostly I think he's worried about Lisa. She's reached out to Tyler a few times recently, but he hasn't spoken to her, and she's pretty upset. She wants things to go back to normal with him, but Tyler doesn't seem interested."

"He's not," Kelsey said.

"Why? I won't tell Bob."

"I don't know exactly. That's what I'm trying to figure out."

"I get it," Morgan said thoughtfully. She twirled a pigtail on her finger. "Another problem we're not going to solve."

"No, this one I definitely don't want to get in the middle of," Kelsey said.

"Yeah, you've already felt the Warrior Queen's wrath." Morgan commented.

Kelsey laughed. "You've heard the nickname too?"

"Who hasn't?" Morgan commented. She leaned back on the sofa. "I miss this. Spending time with you. Having cocoa. Hanging out. Everything seems less complicated."

"I miss that too," Kelsey admitted. "I'm glad to be back home."

"There was a time I couldn't imagine you saying that," Morgan said.

"You mean last week?" Kelsey said. Morgan giggled.

Christmas Eve wasn't considered a holiday at the North house, since generally everyone was so tired from working in the store on the last shopping day before Christmas. So Kelsey and Grandma left Kelsey's exhausted parents at home, and headed over to the Jefferson house for Christmas Eve dinner.

They walked into the kitchen, carrying the fudge that they had made together, and the cookies that Grandma Rose had made alone.

"Welcome, Mrs. North," Mama Jefferson said to Grandma Rose.

"Thank you, Charlene," Grandma said to her.

"Hi, honey," Mama Jefferson said to Kelsey, giving her a hug.

"Hi, Mama," Kelsey replied. She looked around the warm and cozy kitchen and breathed in the delicious scent of gingerbread.

"Hi, Grandma Rose," Jasmine said, hugging Grandma and taking the plate she was carrying.

"Jasmine, it's lovely to see you. You're a grown woman now," Grandma said to Jasmine.

Jasmine beamed. "Thanks, Grandma Rose," she said. "Morgan's here," Jasmine said to Kelsey.

"Jasmine, take our guests to say hello to Papa," Mama Jefferson said.

"Mama, do you need help?" Kelsey asked.

"No, Kelsey. Jasmine and I have it under control," Mama said. Kelsey nodded and followed Jasmine and Grandma out into the living room.

Morgan smiled as they walked into the room. She was sitting next to Papa Jefferson's chair, which he had vacated to greet Grandma Rose. Jace stood up as well.

"Mrs. North, I'm so glad you could come by for a visit," Papa said as Jasmine walked back into the kitchen.

"I appreciate the invitation, Charles. But call me Rose," Grandma said to him.

"Sit, sit," Papa said to her, and Grandma Rose sat in the chair next to Morgan.

"Mrs. North, I'm not sure if you remember me," Jace said to her, coming over to shake her hand.

"Jace," Grandma said with confidence. "You've certainly grown."

Jace smiled as he shook her hand. "Birdbrain," Jace whispered in greeting to Kelsey as he passed by her.

"Jerk," Kelsey replied. Jace pulled up an additional chair and sat next to his father.

"I understand that you're in graduate school, young man?" Grandma said to Jace.

"I'm finishing my thesis, Mrs. North," Jace replied.

"You aren't done with that yet?" Morgan said.

"It's a little more complicated than writing your name... Morgan," Jace replied. Kelsey stifled a laugh. Jace was so used to calling Morgan 'Bonehead', he probably had to pause to remember her real name.

"Jace should be done by the end of the year," Papa Jefferson said pointedly. Jace refused to catch Papa Jefferson's eye.

"I'm sure you'll be fine," Grandma Rose commented.

"Thank you," Jace said politely.

Morgan's phone buzzed. She looked down at it and typed something. Then she clicked it off.

"So, Kelsey, how's work?" Papa Jefferson asked.

"It's great, Papa," Kelsey replied.

"I understand that you're just back from leading a project in Arizona," he commented. Kelsey was about to mention that she was part of a team, but then she realized. There was no reason to downplay her role. She had led the project, successfully.

"Yes, Papa," Kelsey said proudly.

"Very good," Papa Jefferson said, beaming at her. "All of the young women are doing quite well with their careers," he said, glancing at Jace, who wisely was looking away from Papa's direction.

"How is your office doing, Charles?" Grandma Rose.

"We recently hired a new accountant, and of course, we landed a very special client this year," Papa Jefferson said.

"Who?" Kelsey asked curiously.

"You," Jace said snidely. Kelsey looked at him, puzzled, but realized that her father had mentioned that the Jefferson family accounting firm would be handling the accounts for Kelsey's building.

"Right. I forgot," Kelsey commented.

"Too many other things on your mind. Like being sworn into the bar. Congratulations."

"Thanks, Papa," Kelsey said. She had practically forgotten, since she hadn't had time to celebrate.

"Yeah, the pictures were great," Morgan said. "You looked so professional."

Jace looked doubtful.

Jasmine walked into the living room.

"Papa, dinner is served," Jasmine said.

The group headed to the dining room. Kelsey noticed that Morgan and Mama Jefferson had seemed to come to a bit of a truce while Kelsey had been away. They were polite, but Kelsey could tell that neither one of them was particularly excited to spend time with the other. Jasmine's husband Jim arrived a few minutes late, but was forgiven as he had been finishing up work.

After a wonderful meal of chicken with pesto, they all returned to the living room. As Jasmine and Kelsey passed out cookies, the doorbell rang.

"Morgan, could you get that?" Mama asked as she poured tea for Grandma Rose.

"Sure," Morgan said, standing. She walked over to the front door and opened it. Kelsey glanced over. A young man in a suit, who Kelsey didn't recognize, was standing at the door. He spoke to Morgan for a moment.

As Jace took a cookie off of the plate, Morgan shouted, "Wow!" And she ran out of the front door, past the young man.

"Morgan?" Papa said, quizzically.

Kelsey set the cookie plate down on the table and walked over to the front door, where the young man had stepped to the side. Everyone else followed Kelsey, curiously.

In the dark, Kelsey could see a sports car parked in front of the Jefferson house. A second car, lights on, sat across the street. Morgan had opened the driver's side door of the sports car and was getting in.

"Morgan, what are you doing?" Kelsey asked.

"Get in, Kelsey!" Morgan shouted, before closing the door. Kelsey ran out to the car and opened the passenger door. She slid into the seat, and barely had closed the door before Morgan floored the gas pedal.

"Wait, wait, I don't have my seatbelt on," Kelsey said, as she pulled it from the side. She fastened it and looked at Morgan, who looked ecstatic as they drove toward the lagoon. "What's going on? Whose car is this?" she asked.

"Mine!" Morgan replied happily.

Kelsey looked around the car, but in the dark, she couldn't tell anything about it except that it was brand new.

"Hang on," Morgan said. She shifted gears and they sped down the hill.

"Did Bob buy this for you?" Kelsey asked, as Morgan turned right on Kearney, then took a left on Blaine.

"Yes! Merry Christmas to me," Morgan replied as they zipped down the street.

Morgan and Kelsey returned to the Jefferson house less than ten minutes later, having looped around Discovery Road.

"What a ride," Morgan said, as she got out of the car. Kelsey agreed. It had been a while since she had driven with Morgan, who made Ryan's driving seem conservative. Kelsey got out of the car and closed the door. Jace opened the front door of the house, and looked out.

"They're back," he called into the house, and he walked out to the car.

"Corvette," he said, as he reached the girls.

"It's awesome," Morgan said.

"Let me drive it," Jace said to Morgan.

"Are you going to keep calling me Bonehead?" she asked.

Kelsey could see Jace as he thought in the dark.

"I'll give you a week off," he said.

"Done," Morgan said. She threw him the keys, and he caught them. "Make sure it comes back in one piece. I know where you live," she said.

"You should be worrying about yourself," Jace commented. "The argument's already started."

Morgan looked at Kelsey. "Maybe I'll go home," she said.

"You've got to face it sometime," Kelsey replied. "Jace, what's the score?"

"Two to two. Jim's abstaining," Jace said as he got into the car.

"Who's on my side?" Morgan asked, but Jace didn't hear.

"Papa and Grandma Rose," Kelsey said. She knew her grandmother well enough to know that she wouldn't be against Morgan taking a car from her billionaire boyfriend.

Morgan sighed as they headed back into the open door of the Jefferson house.

"Did you enjoy your new toy?" Mama Jefferson asked Morgan, sharply.

"Charlene," Papa said, wearily.

"What kind is it?" Grandma Rose asked Morgan.

"Corvette," Morgan said. She sat in a chair and took a cookie from the plate.

"And what did you do for it?" Mama Jefferson asked. Kelsey looked at her in surprise, but Morgan answered.

"Forgave," Morgan snapped. Kelsey knew that Morgan was referring to Fiona, but she understood Morgan's unspoken message. Mama Jefferson was supposed to forgive too. But Kelsey was confident that she wouldn't.

"It's really pretty," Grandma said. "Red?" It was difficult to tell in the dark.

"Yes," Morgan said.

Kelsey glanced at Jasmine, who was silent. But she didn't look happy either. Kelsey assumed that Jace was right, and that they had simply missed Jasmine's part in the argument.

"Where's Jace?" Jim asked, in an attempt to break the ice.

"He wanted to take a ride," Morgan said.

"I suppose he wasn't the only one," Jasmine said, sarcastically.

Morgan stood up and glared at Jasmine. "That's it. I'm sick of you." And she walked out of the house.

Papa Jefferson looked at his daughter, angrily.

"Jasmine. We have guests in our home, and that's the way you speak in front of them," he said sharply.

"I'm sorry, Grandma Rose," Jasmine said softly.

"We should go," Kelsey said to Grandma. Kelsey knew that Grandma saw the look in her eyes, because Grandma stood up more quickly than Kelsey knew she could.

"It's been fun," Grandma said to Papa Jefferson, who didn't look amused at all.

"It was very nice to see you," he said. "Let me see you out," he added, standing and escorting Grandma Rose to the door. Kelsey followed them.

"I'm sorry for what happened this evening, Rose."

"It's OK, Charles. Morgan seems to be a lightning rod in this town."

"That she is," Papa Jefferson said, glancing back into his now-silent house.

Grandma Rose gave him a gentle smile. "Merry Christmas, Charles," she said.

"Thank you. Merry Christmas to you, too," he said. Kelsey took her grandmother's arm, and they headed toward the street.

"Merry Christmas, Papa," Kelsey called as they reached the sidewalk.

"Merry Christmas, Kelsey," he replied. Papa Jefferson gave them a final glance, then he shut the door of his house.

"Well, I want a ride in Morgan's car," Grandma Rose said excitedly. "Where do you think Jace went with it?"

"If he's smart, out of town," Kelsey replied. "Let's go home. You can see it tomorrow."

They headed down the street, towards Kelsey's house. As they got within seeing distance of the house, Kelsey saw Morgan standing on the path leading to the door.

"Back so soon?" Morgan quipped.

"The party was less exciting without you there," Kelsey replied. Morgan laughed loudly.

"You girls have fun," Grandma Rose, said, heading up the path. "Morgan, I want you to take me for a drive tomorrow."

"You bet, Grandma Rose," Morgan said.

"I'll see you in a while, Grandma," Kelsey said.

"Don't hurry, Kelsey. I might go to bed. Big day tomorrow," Grandma Rose replied.

"OK. Good night," Kelsey said.

"Good night, dears," Grandma said. The girls watched as Grandma walked the rest of the way to the door and let herself in.

"Now what?" Kelsey asked Morgan.

"Now we wait for my new car," Morgan replied.

The girls sat outside Kelsey's house, talking. About fifteen minutes later, Jace roared up and parked the car. He got out and walked up to the girls. Jace handed Morgan the keys.

"I figured you'd be here," he said to her. "What did I miss?"

"You can imagine," Kelsey replied.

"I sure can. Merry Christmas, Birdbrain. And Morgan."

Morgan laughed. "Merry Christmas, Jace," she said, as Jace ambled back toward his house.

Morgan twirled the keys in her hand. "Do you want a car?" Morgan asked Kelsey. "My old one?" she explained.

"Give it to Carly," Kelsey replied. "She could use it."

"Good idea," Morgan said. She ran her hand through her hair. "Can I leave this one here tonight? I'll drive the other one home tomorrow, and Carly can give me a ride back."

"I don't see why not," Kelsey said. "You're taking the risk that my mother spray-paints it while you're gone, though."

Morgan giggled. "She won't be the only one, once the story gets around town."

"Poor you," Kelsey said.

"I don't know. I got a Corvette for Christmas. It beats the school supplies I used to get this time of year," Morgan replied.

"Good point," Kelsey agreed.

"All right," Morgan said, standing and brushing off her jeans. "Time to figure out how to tell my dad about my new car."

"You've got all night," Kelsey replied, standing next to her.

"I'll need it," Morgan replied. "Do you want me to leave you the keys?"

"No," Kelsey said. "I don't want to wake up to the sound of Grandma burning rubber."

"OK," Morgan said, giving Kelsey a hug. "I'll see you tomorrow."

"See you, Morgan," Kelsey said, and Morgan headed back down the street to pick up her old car. Once she was out of view, Kelsey walked into her own house.

The house was silent. Kelsey guessed that Grandma had gone to bed, just like she knew her parents had. Kelsey locked the front door, and quietly walked up to her room.

She got dressed in her pajamas, and settled into her bed. She glanced at her phone, and as she expected, there was a message from Tyler.

"I wonder whose car is outside?" Kelly North said, as she sat on the sofa on Christmas morning.

Grandma and Kelsey glanced guiltily at each other.

"Someone must be visiting the Coopers," Dan North replied. "So, Kels, are you the Christmas elf?"

"Come on, Dad. I'm a lawyer now," Kelsey groaned.

"You're still our little girl," her father said.

"Fine," Kelsey said unwillingly. She put her coffee cup on the end table and walked over to the Christmas tree.

"My gift first, Kelsey," Grandma Rose said. Kelsey felt a prick of anxiety. Grandma's gift last year had created a battle which led to an argument, Tyler being kicked out of the North house, and Kelsey running after him. But of course, Tyler wasn't here this year.

"OK," Kelsey said, picking up the gift her grandmother had brought. She looked at the tag in surprise. Grandma Rose had only placed one gift under the tree. "Mom. It's for you," Kelsey said, handing the small box to her mother.

Kelsey's mother looked as surprised as Kelsey felt. She took the box and looked over at her mother-in-law.

"Thank you, Rose," she said. She opened the wrapped box carefully, as Kelsey looked on. She opened the box, and inside was a ruby ring.

"Rose, it's beautiful," Kelly North said, pulling the ring out of the box.

"It's been in our family for generations," Grandma Rose said. "I haven't worn it in years, so I thought someone should get some use out of it."

Kelsey knew it was the perfect gift for her mother, who loved jewelry.

"Thank you," Kelly North said sincerely, as her husband beamed.

"It's my pleasure," Grandma Rose replied.

To Kelly North's surprise, the ring fit perfectly. It turned out that her husband had arranged for it to be resized for her. Kelsey's mother kissed him.

"Thank you, Dan," she said happily.

"What's the next gift?" Grandma Rose asked eagerly.

"Ready, Grandma?" Kelsey asked quietly a while later. "Morgan's here."

"I'm ready," Grandma said, standing up in the guest room. She joined Kelsey and they left the room and headed downstairs.

"I wish we could distract them," Grandma said.

"I know," Kelsey said.

"Where's Morgan?"

"Outside. She messaged me," Kelsey said. Thanks to her relationship with Bob, Morgan didn't feel particularly comfortable around Kelly North. Of course, after last night, Morgan also wasn't likely to be visiting the Jeffersons anytime soon. With the gift of the car, it was clear that the fragile truce was over.

"Should we tell them we're leaving?" Grandma asked.

Kelsey shook her head. "Let's pretend we went on a walk," Kelsey said, opening the front door.

"Kelsey?" Her mother called.

"Oh, no," Kelsey said under her breath. "Yes?" she called out.

"Are you going out?"

"Yeah, Grandma and I were going for a walk," Kelsey lied.

"I thought you might be heading to the store."

"Not right now. Did you need something?"

"I didn't buy enough eggs, and I wanted to make omelets tomorrow."

"I might go out later," Kelsey replied. She glanced outside. Morgan was looking at them, probably wondering what was going on.

"If you do, I'll take a dozen. Thanks."

"No problem," Kelsey said. And she and her grandmother left. They walked outside to the bright red car that Morgan was leaning against.

"Cool," Grandma Rose said.

"Isn't it," Morgan said excitedly. "Get in, Grandma."

"What about Kelsey?" Grandma said. "I want to sit in the front."

Kelsey noticed something that she had missed in last night's excitement. The Corvette Stingray only had two seats.

"I'll wait here," Kelsey said.

"You told your mother we were going on a walk," Grandma pointed out.

"I'll go on a walk. I'll meet you at Morgan's," Kelsey said.

"Sounds like a plan. Let's go," Morgan said.

Kelsey helped her grandmother get into the car, and Morgan roared off.

Just as Kelsey was about to head off the property and start the short walk to downtown, her father called out to her.

"Hey, Kels."

"Hi, Dad," Kelsey said.

"Your mother said you and your grandmother were going on a walk."

"Morgan drove up, so she and Grandma decided to drive."

"I see," Dan North said doubtfully. "I didn't hear Morgan's car." He looked at the empty spot where Morgan's new car had been parked, in front of their house. "In fact, the only car I heard was the distinctive sound of a Corvette."

"Really?" Kelsey said, but she knew her father wasn't fooled.

"Morgan's Christmas gift?" he asked.

"Yeah," Kelsey admitted.

"Oh, boy," Dan North said.

"You might not want to tell Mom."

"She's going to find out."

"Of course she will. Morgan got it last night when we were at the Jeffersons'. I just said that you might not want to be the one to tell her," Kelsey replied.

"That's probably true," he mused. "So last night wasn't the peaceful dinner that I had imagined."

"Be grateful that you weren't there," Kelsey said.

"How bad was it?"

"Morgan walked out, Jasmine got into trouble, and we left early," Kelsey replied.

"So better than expected?"

Kelsey laughed. "Yeah, I guess you could say that."

"It's like we have our own soap opera."

"And Morgan is the star," Kelsey said.

"Unfortunately for her," Dan North said.

"Did you have a nice Christmas, Grandma?" Kelsey asked as she drove onto Route 20 on Tuesday. They had an hour-long trip ahead of them, back to Port Angeles.

"It was wonderful, Kelsey. I always enjoy visiting Port Townsend."

Kelsey wondered how her grandmother would feel about living there, but she thought she'd let her parents handle that particular question when the time came.

"Did you get everything you wanted?" Grandma asked.

Kelsey considered the question. She missed Tyler, and their messages over the holiday had done nothing to alleviate her desire to see him. But January 2nd was just around the corner.

"I did," Kelsey replied, as a SUV passed them on the road.

"Did you mind that I gave my ring to your mother?" Grandma asked.

"No, of course not," Kelsey said. She didn't wear a lot of jewelry, and anyway, eventually Kelly would give it to Kelsey.

"You're a young woman, and I'm confident that soon you'll be getting a ring of your own," Grandma commented. Kelsey glanced at her grandmother, but Grandma Rose was looking out of the window as they drove through the Olympic Peninsula. Kelsey wasn't sure what to say to that, so she remained silent. They were quiet for a few moments, then Grandma Rose asked,

"How do you like living in Seattle?"

"It's great. You should come visit me," Kelsey said.

"I was there for your graduation," Grandma pointed out.

"So was everyone. It should just be you and me for a weekend," Kelsey said.

"Getting into trouble?" Grandma asked.

Kelsey giggled. "Always," she replied.

"I have a feeling your parents wouldn't approve that trip," Grandma commented.

"Since when do you listen to my parents?" Kelsey asked.

"Well, Kelsey, I'm getting older, so I kind of have to listen to them now," Grandma said. "Your father had to listen to me during the first part of his life, and I have to listen to him during the last part of mine."

Kelsey frowned. "You're going to live forever," she said with determination.

"I hope so too, darling." Grandma Rose chuckled. "I hope so," And she looked out of the window again.

A little more than an hour later, Kelsey stood next to the car, which was sitting in the parking lot of the Port Angeles Safeway. The remains of a peanut butter cookie were in her hand, and tears were streaming down her cheeks.

The sadness had caught her by surprise. She had walked her grandmother to the door of the apartment, and Kelsey had given her a long hug. Then Kelsey had got in the car, driven the minute-long trip to Safeway to get a snack for the ride back, and in the middle of the parking lot, the tears had begun to fall.

"Hi, honey," Kelsey's mother said as she walked into the North house that evening. Kelsey turned her head. She had been in the living room, reading.

"Thanks for driving your grandmother back," Kelsey's father said. He sat next to her, as Kelly walked through the living room and up the stairs. "Your mother said that you were worried about her."

"A little," Kelsey said.

Her father nodded thoughtfully. "She's healthy."

"I know," Kelsey said. "She told me the doctor said she would live longer than him."

"So why are you worried?"

Kelsey thought about her answer before she spoke.

"Because she's always been on my side," she replied.

Her father smiled. "That she has," he replied. "You could set our house on fire, and there would be Rose, standing there with marshmallows for the two of you to roast."

Her father spoke the truth. Rose North had always been Kelsey's biggest fan, and Kelsey was afraid of being without her.

"Kelsey, you never know how long you're going to have with someone, so you have to make the most of the time that you have."

"I don't have a lot of time with Grandma any more," Kelsey commented.

"I know. But she understands. You're beginning to build a life for yourself, and you need to do that right now."

"I wonder if I'll regret it later. Not spending more time with her."

"Of course you will," her father said, and it surprised her. "We always regret the road we took, and glorify the road not taken. That's part of being an adult, you have to make choices. And for every choice you take, there's thousands you give up. Just do the best you can."

"Maybe Grandma could come spend a weekend with me in Seattle?" Kelsey asked.

"I bet she'd like that," her father said. "Should I make sure I have bail money ready?"

Kelsey grinned. "Definitely," she replied.

The rest of the time at home was quiet without Grandma Rose around. Kelsey had lunch with Morgan at Ben's Cafe, which to Kelsey's surprise was even more crowded than it had been this summer. She went to the Jefferson house to have dinner with Mama and Papa, but it was thankfully drama-free. They spent most of the visit discussing Kelsey's job and debating various investments for Kelsey's rapidly-accumulating money.

Kelsey worked in the store for a couple of days, but because Christmas was over, she mostly spent the time hanging jackets, cleaning shelves, and talking to her father. And on the day before she left, Kelsey and Morgan had another sleepover at Morgan's condo.

"So, Kels, what are you doing tonight?" Kelsey's father asked, as he casually leaned in her doorway.

"Tonight? Right, it's New Year's Eve," Kelsey said. She had pretty much forgotten, since her mind was on returning to work on January 2nd. "Probably nothing," she admitted. It was Ryan's birthday today, and Ryan and Jessica's first anniversary, so although they were back from L.A., she didn't expect that she would see Jess and Ryan for a while.

"That's a little sad. You should go out."

"I don't think I will," Kelsey said, her ponytail brushing her neck as she put her sweatshirt in her bag.

"I thought you were invited to a fireworks party tonight. Why don't you go to that?" her father asked.

Kelsey glanced at her father. Bill Simon, in fact, had invited her and the entire office to see the fireworks from the law office of one of his friends, whose building had a spectacular view of the Space Needle. But Kelsey didn't remember mentioning the invitation to her father.

"Why?"

"Because it's a few blocks away from your apartment. And because you're too young to stay in on New Year's Eve."

"Dad," Kelsey protested.

"Seriously, it's pathetic. Promise me you'll go."

"What?" Kelsey said.

"Promise me. I don't want to think I'm having more fun on New Year's Eve than my daughter is," Dan North insisted.

Kelsey sighed dramatically. "I'll think about it," she said, but her father gave her a look. "Fine, fine, I'll go," Kelsey said in defeat. So much for sitting at home in her jammies with a cup of warm cocoa.

"Great. I'll let you finish packing," her father said delightedly, and he left the room.

Kelsey glanced at the clock on her phone a few hours after her father had dropped her off at her Seattle home. 10:50 p.m. She sighed, took a sip of cocoa, and put her Kindle on the coffee table. She slowly and a little unwillingly got up. Not for the first time she wondered why her father had insisted that she leave her cozy apartment and head out, just to watch the fireworks.

Then again, it felt a little pathetic to Kelsey to spend New Year's Eve sitting on the sofa, watching the fireworks on TV, despite the fact that was exactly what she wanted to do.

She stood for a moment, debating whether she could come up with a good enough excuse for her father so she wouldn't feel guilty about not going out.

Kelsey decided that she could not. So she walked into the bedroom to change.

Kelsey stepped into the party thirty minutes later. Since she was technically going to a law office, she had taken the time to put her hair up in a chignon and put on a navy-blue dress. There would be a lot of lawyers here tonight, and as always, she wanted to maintain a professional appearance around her peers, even on New Year's Eve. It was warm enough to leave her coat behind, so she had done so.

As she expected, the Baker and Hamilton law office was host to a large number of people, since it had a wonderful view of the fireworks. As a concession to herself, Kelsey had decided to come late and leave early. But at least she could tell her father she had attended.

Kelsey looked around the room, and spotted Bill Simon, who was talking with a fellow lawyer. He had a club soda in his hand, and they were deep in conversation, so Kelsey decided not to interrupt. Instead, she headed over to the buffet table. Within minutes, she was in conversation with a lawyer who had previously been at Collins Nicol, but was now working for the law firm she was standing in. He had left before Kelsey had been unceremoniously fired, so Kelsey didn't bother to enlighten him about why she wasn't at Collins anymore.

She walked over and said hi to Bill, who had finished his conversation. Kelsey realized that she hadn't seen Tyler. She supposed he had decided not to come to the office to see the fireworks. Perhaps he was celebrating Ryan's birthday tonight.

After a conversation with Millie, who had also decided that it was pathetic to stay at home, and a conversation with Kevin Hamilton, one of the partners of the firm hosting the party, who had introduced himself to her, it was time for the fireworks.

Kelsey stood near the window, and everyone who had been milling around began moving toward the window to make sure that they had a good view. Millie and Bill were standing on the other side of the large set of windows, talking. As Kelsey looked out at the Space Needle, she realized how happy she was to be back in Seattle, after almost two months away.

Suddenly, she heard the people around her counting.

"Ten, nine, eight, seven, six, five, four, three!"

"Kelsey," a familiar voice said behind her.

Kelsey turned around and looked up into Tyler's brown eyes. It had been so long since she had seen him, and her heart jolted.

"Two, one! Happy New Year!" the crowd shouted.

Tyler took Kelsey's face into his hands and kissed her deeply. Although her back was to the Space Needle, all Kelsey could feel were fireworks.

"Did you bring a coat?" Tyler asked her as the fireworks continued behind her. Kelsey shook her head as she looked at him in shock. He kissed her again, then Tyler took her hand and silently walked her out of the party.

Tyler kept kissing her, as they waited for the elevator, once they were on it, once they reached the lobby. He kept kissing her, and Kelsey kissed him back. It was like they had never stopped, and she never wanted to stop again.

Tyler led her out to the street, and out into the cool air. He kissed her hand.

"I'd say that I don't know what came over me, but it would be a lie. I've missed you so much, Kelsey."

"I missed you too," Kelsey said. Tyler caressed her hand gently as they slowly walked down University Street.

"I want you back," he said simply.

Kelsey stopped abruptly on the sidewalk and let go of Tyler's hand.

"What do you mean?" she said. She was still stunned from his kisses, but despite this, Kelsey's mind was still clear.

"Exactly what I said. I love you, Kelsey."

"You broke up with me," she replied. The orange glow of the street lights shone on them in the dark.

"You know I had no choice," Tyler said, looking at her. "I had to protect you."

Kelsey was silent and Tyler continued.

"I had to make sure you finished school and passed the bar. I wanted to have this conversation with you six weeks ago, after we were sworn in, but of course Bill Simon sent you away. I've been going crazy waiting for you to come back." Tyler paused.

"I asked you to wait, and now the waiting is over," he said. He took her hand again, and they resumed walking.

"Why are things different now?" Kelsey asked cautiously.

"Because there's nothing Lisa can take from you. Bill would fire me faster than he would let you leave, and you've passed the bar. You're a lawyer."

Kelsey felt a flicker of hope, but she willed her mind to extinguish it. Despite the fact that she had wanted Tyler to fight for her, that she wanted him to find a way for them to be together again, she couldn't help but be wary. They crossed Sixth Avenue.

"Tyler, your mother tried to ruin my life because I was dating you."

"I know. And there wasn't anything I could do about it then. But there's a lot I can do about it now. Kelsey, there was too much at stake before. Your grades, the bar application, your parents' store. I couldn't risk your future. I had to let you go."

"And now you want me back."

"I wanted you then. I couldn't have you."

"And what will you do when she tries to ruin me again?"

"She won't. I have a plan. I'm not letting you go."

"Tyler…" Kelsey began, but then she was silent. Her heart wouldn't let her mind voice any doubts at all. She had waited too long. Desired him for too long.

"Please don't say no to me, Kelsey. I've never wanted anything or anyone as much as I've wanted you," Tyler said.

As they waited for the light on Fifth Avenue, Kelsey considered what Tyler was saying to her. Tyler stood quietly.

"I don't know what to say to you," Kelsey finally admitted as the light changed. They didn't move from the corner.

"Tell me that you love me," Tyler replied.

Kelsey felt tears come to her eyes.

"Tell me that you can't live without me like I can't live without you. Tell me that we'll never be apart again," Tyler continued. "Tell me that you love me."

Kelsey stood silently for a moment. Finally, she nodded.

"I love you, Tyler," she said, tears running down her face. "I love you so much," she said in a whisper. Tyler took her face in his hands, and he kissed her once again.

A few minutes later, Kelsey sat in a chair in the lobby bar of the Fairmont Olympic Hotel. The lobby sparkled with holiday lights even at this late hour, and although they were the only patrons, the piano played softly.

Kelsey's eyes took in what seemed to be hundreds of white roses that graced the area around her. She had been to the Fairmont with Tyler more times than she could remember, but she had never seen so many flowers, and the effect was stunning. She supposed it was for the New Year.

Tyler sat in one of the brown leather chairs across from her and Kelsey wondered what it would be like to be his girlfriend again. To go on dates and spend time together. She looked at his handsome face and smiled.

"Thank you," Tyler said to the server, who had taken their drinks order. The server nodded politely and walked away.

Kelsey looked at Tyler, who was looking thoughtfully at the table between them.

Tyler stood, walked over to her chair, and leaned down, kissing her again. He stood next to her for a moment, holding her hand, and Kelsey felt his warmth.

"So I have a question for you," he said quietly.

"OK," Kelsey said, looking up at him. Tyler knelt next to her chair. He looked into her eyes, and Kelsey looked back at him. It was nice to be so close to him again.

Tyler gently let go of her hand and reached into his suit jacket pocket.

"Kelsey, will you marry me?" Tyler asked, pulling out a dark blue jewelry box. He opened the box and took out a stunning diamond ring.

Kelsey watched him in disbelief, as Tyler gently took her hand and placed the ring on her finger, where it sparkled in the light.

Her heart was pounding, and she couldn't breathe. It was if time were standing still, silently waiting for her to speak.

Ever since Tyler had kissed her, Kelsey had been trying to process everything Tyler had said to her.

That he wanted her back.

That she would be safe.

That he would protect her.

And that he loved her.

She looked into his eyes as he patiently waited for her answer, waiting for her, as she had waited for him, with love and respect.

With hope.

Everything was a blur since she had first seen him tonight, and her mind was racing to catch up.

But finally she understood.

Tyler's eyes hadn't left her face. Kelsey took a deep breath, then shouted,

"Yes!"

She threw her arms around him and Tyler hugged her tightly. She closed her eyes, and Tyler rested his head next to hers as the staff applauded.

Their ordered drinks never arrived. Instead, the beaming waiter arrived with a bottle of sparkling cider and two champagne glasses. Overwhelmed with joy, Kelsey slowly realized that the entire staff of the Fairmont was in on Tyler's secret as she was presented with a bouquet of red roses, and the couple had their picture taken with Tyler's new phone.

They were congratulated by the hotel manager and after a few more pictures, and more than a few kisses, Tyler and Kelsey left the hotel and headed back out to University Street.

Kelsey looked at the ring as the lights surrounding the hotel driveway shone on them. It was princess cut, on a platinum band.

"Do you like it?" Tyler asked.

"It's beautiful," Kelsey said.

"Like the bride-to-be." Tyler replied. He kissed her on the lips.

Kelsey sighed. "It's too late to call my parents."

"They already know," Tyler replied. Kelsey looked at Tyler in surprise.

"I asked your Dad for permission when I was in New York," Tyler said.

"Wow," Kelsey said. Tyler kissed her hand.

Kelsey bit her lip. "Can we really do this?" she asked.

Tyler looked amused. "It's done," he replied happily.

Kelsey had a million questions for Tyler. But instead of asking, she walked with him toward the waterfront silently. All of the questions came back to the same ones. How were they going to get married when Lisa Olsen was still against it? Was it really true that they could be together? She decided to put all her questions aside and enjoy the moment. Who knew how long it would last?

"Can I stay?" Tyler asked Kelsey as he stood at her doorway a few minutes later. It was the first time he had walked into her building, the first time he had been at her door. "On the sofa," Tyler clarified. "I can't bear to let you out of my sight."

Kelsey gave him a smile. "Come in, Tyler," she said, and they walked into the apartment.

"I'm going to change," Kelsey said to him. Tyler nodded, and didn't take his eyes off of her.

"What is it?" Kelsey asked.

"You have no idea how much I missed you," Tyler said.

Kelsey walked over and gave him a kiss. But to her surprise, he put his arms around her and pulled her tightly towards himself.

"I love you, Kelsey," he said softly. He kissed her hair.

"I love you too, Tyler," Kelsey replied, kissing him back.

She left a few minutes later, then returned wearing fleece pants and her Portland State sweatshirt. Tyler had draped his jacket over a chair and was sitting on the sofa, in the dark. He had turned off the lights. Kelsey joined him, and he put his arms around her. He nuzzled her ear and ran his hand down her arm.

Kelsey cuddled up next to him. It had been so long, yet it felt like yesterday that they had been together like this, wrapped in each other's arms, so in love.

Their love hadn't gone, but it had changed. Kelsey knew it would be stronger, because now they would have to fight for it. Tyler had clearly thrown down the gauntlet by asking Kelsey to take him back, and now they would have to see what awaited them. But Kelsey was no longer afraid of dragons. Even those named Lisa Olsen.

Tyler pulled Kelsey closer and sighed happily. Kelsey rested her head on his chest and they sat silently for a moment.

"Are you tired?" Tyler asked.

"No," Kelsey replied. "Are you?"

"No."

Kelsey looked at him and gave him a kiss on the cheek. Tyler smiled and kissed her on the lips. Kelsey placed her head gently back on his chest.

"How was your vacation?" she asked, to distract herself from asking her other questions. The ones she was worried about the answers to.

"Better now," Tyler replied.

"What did you do?" Kelsey asked.

"Thought about you," Tyler replied.

"Really, Tyler."

"I'm being honest," Tyler replied.

"You must have done something else," Kelsey replied. "For example, I'm guessing you bought a ring," she said, holding her hand up.

"I did," Tyler replied.

"Thank you."

"Thank you for saying yes."

"You knew I would. I promised you," Kelsey replied.

"I guess I did," Tyler said. "But thank you anyway."

"Thank you for asking."

"It took long enough," Tyler replied.

"It wasn't your fault," Kelsey replied.

"I suppose," Tyler said.

"So what else did you do?" Kelsey asked, getting back to the subject.

"Liz and I went to Vermont."

"Vermont?" Kelsey asked.

"Liz hadn't left the city for a while and she had some friends up there with a cabin. We stayed with them."

"Was it pretty?"

"Very. Lots of snow."

"Did you go skiing?"

"We did," Tyler replied. He kissed Kelsey's hair.

"What else did you do?"

"We stopped by Boston to have lunch with Sophia and Cindy," Tyler said.

"How was that?"

"It was good. And I got to show Liz around Harvard."

"So what was it like to hang out with Liz?" Kelsey asked.

"Fun," Tyler replied. "Except when we were discussing Chris."

"Did he come up a lot?"

"A few times. I wasn't surprised. They had been going out for a really long time, and they still see each other sometimes."

"Really? Why?"

"They have a lot of the same friends, and Liz is an art professor. That's how she met Chris. They run in the same circles."

"Is that hard for her?" Kelsey asked.

"I think so," Tyler replied. Kelsey didn't press him. She knew that Tyler felt responsible for the breakup, and although he might not be concerned about Chris's feelings, he would care about Liz's.

They sat quietly, then Tyler asked, "And how was your Christmas, Mrs.-Olsen-to-be?"

Kelsey couldn't help but smile at the name.

"Annoying. But you knew that. I was in Port Townsend without you, and with Jace."

Tyler laughed. "How was that?"

"Better than expected, since my grandmother was also there for a week. But still annoying."

"I'm sorry."

"Don't be. Just don't let me go by myself any more."

"I promise," Tyler said, hugging her tightly.

"We'll suffer together," Kelsey said.

"I could never suffer with you," Tyler said.

"You've obviously forgotten about my mother," Kelsey quipped.

Tyler laughed again. "I'll have to win her over before the wedding," he said.

"Yeah, good luck with that," Kelsey replied. Tyler moved one arm, stroked her hair, and placed his arm back around her. Kelsey cuddled up against him again. The lights of the city twinkled outside of the window.

Kelsey thought about what Tyler had said, and remembered that he had mentioned Sophia. There was something she had been wondering about since graduation, but she had never asked him.

"Why did Sophia write your graduation speech?" she asked.

"You noticed."

"I did."

"My speech was no longer relevant, and I wasn't in any condition to write another one. So I asked Sophia to write one for me."

"No longer relevant?" Kelsey asked him. "What do you mean?"

"Would you like to hear it?" Tyler asked her.

"I would."

"*E pluribus unum*," Tyler began from memory. "'Out of many, one'. It's on our money, and as new lawyers, money might seem like the only reason that the phrase is relevant to our lives. But I would like us to consider the possibility that as lawyers, *E pluribus unum* is more important than meets the eye.

"We have a new duty to our community. To do good work, to bill fairly, to lead our clients to the path of justice, because that's what the larger community asks of us. When we are sworn into the bar, we will be asked to remember our responsibility in all things. And this is where '*E pluribus unum*' comes in.

"Out of the many graduates here, we need to have one goal. To make the world a better place than we find it. At times in our careers, we will be asked to do the wrong thing. To cut corners, to make unfair choices, even to tell lies. But if we remember that out of the many of us, we are creating one legal community, we'll be able to make the right decisions for ourselves, and for the larger world.

"A similar sentiment can be found in the Bible. Genesis 2:24. *E duobus unum*. Out of two, one. But in the Bible it reads, 'A man leaves his father and mother, and is united to his wife, and they become one."

Tyler paused, and hugged Kelsey.

"Kelsey Anne North, will you marry me?"

Kelsey put her hand over her mouth in shock. She broke out of Tyler's arms and looked at him in the darkened room.

"You were going to ask me to marry you at graduation?" she asked.

"I was. But I couldn't," he said. "So I asked Sophia to help me."

"You really were going to ask me to marry you then?" Kelsey said.

"Of course. That's why I insisted we go to Port Townsend at spring break. So I could ask Dan for permission to marry you." Tyler put his arms back around her and pulled her gently back into his chest.

"You told Dad?" Kelsey said in amazement.

"Yes. Then two days later I told him I had to break up with you."

Kelsey thought back to their spring break. Now she understood the worried look on her father's face as she had left Port Townsend.

"I've wanted you to be my wife for a long time, Kelsey," Tyler said. "I'm not giving you up."

Kelsey glanced at him, and she wiped her eyes. "When did you write the speech?" she asked.

"The weekend I found out I was going to be the editor of Law Review," Tyler replied.

"You are serious about me," Kelsey commented.

"I always have been. I just haven't always communicated it well to you," Tyler replied. "But you know now. And you won't forget."

"Never," Kelsey replied, cuddling against him again.

They sat together on the sofa silently, Kelsey secure in Tyler's arms. She closed her eyes and realized that for the first time, in a very long time, she was at peace.

A few hours later, Tyler once again stood in her doorway, this time wearing a green fleece and jeans. He was holding a large manila envelope.

Last night they had fallen asleep on the sofa together, and Kelsey had woken up covered with the blanket he had bought for her at Kalaloch, and a note sat in the arms of one of teddy bears Jasmine had given her. Tyler had written that he'd be back to take her to breakfast.

"Good morning, Princess," he said, kissing her as Kelsey opened the door.

"Hi, Tyler," she replied.

Tyler walked into the apartment. "Nice view," he said, looking out of the window.

"Thank you for arranging it," Kelsey replied as she put on her fleece jacket. She zipped it up, as Tyler watched her thoughtfully.

Tyler put his arms around Kelsey and kissed her gently. Kelsey leaned her head against him once more. They stood together, holding each other silently. There were no words that needed to be said.

Kelsey felt the quiet movement of Tyler's chest as he breathed, and her body moved in sync with his, rising and falling as she delighted in being wrapped in his arms once again.

Tyler kissed her hair. "I never want to be away from you again," he said to her, rubbing her arm softly with his hand.

"Me, neither," Kelsey agreed.

"And we aren't going to be apart again," Tyler said decisively. "But we need to go to Ryan's now. We have some things to discuss."

"OK," Kelsey said. Kelsey wondered what Jessica would think about seeing Tyler, but she didn't say anything.

"Are you ready to go?" Tyler asked.

"I am," Kelsey replied. She moved to leave his arms, but Tyler held onto her tightly.

"Not yet," Tyler said, and he hugged her once more.

As the winter sun warmed the now-cold January air, Kelsey and Tyler walked down First Avenue towards Ryan and Jessica's condo. They held hands. Tyler walked on Kelsey's right, closest to the street as he usually did, and Kelsey's new ring shone on her left hand, and every few moments she peeked at it again.

It was stunning in its simplicity, and exactly the kind of engagement ring she would have picked for herself. Her ring was nothing like Jessica's enormous one, but instead something that she would feel comfortable wearing to work.

"How was Arizona?" Tyler asked as they passed Pike Place Market.

"No idea. I spent all my time working," Kelsey replied.

"That's a surprise," Tyler said sarcastically.

"I didn't mind," Kelsey said.

"You have a good attitude about work," Tyler replied. "I don't."

"No?" Kelsey said.

"No. Bill called me a spoiled brat last week. I'm starting to think he's right."

"You never minded studying," Kelsey said.

"True. I find work more difficult when I calculate my hourly wage," Tyler said.

"Think of all you're learning," Kelsey commented.

"I try. It's difficult at 3 a.m. when I'm sitting at my desk. It will be easier now though."

"Why?"

"Because you're with me," Tyler said, kissing her.

"What are you working on? Ryan said you worked on Thanksgiving Day."

"I worked to avoid going to Medina," Tyler replied. "I'll tell you what I'm working on at Ryan's. Did you have fun with Ryan and Jess?"

"I did. It was nice not having to be alone. I made them work for Simon too," Kelsey said.

"You say that I work a lot, but so do you. Did you work at your parents' store during Christmas?" Tyler asked.

"I did. In fact, I enjoyed working in my new building in Port Townsend. Do you want it back?"

Tyler laughed. "No. It's yours. I promised to break up with you. I didn't promise not to get back together with you later."

"You're quite the lawyer, Mr. Olsen," Kelsey said.

"Thank you."

"I'm not sure that's a compliment," Kelsey said.

"I'll take any loophole I can to have you back in my life. I missed being your boyfriend," Tyler kissed her hair.

"I missed you too," Kelsey said. "I never thought you'd come back to me."

Tyler looked at her in surprise.

"You didn't say how long I had to wait," Kelsey commented.

"You waited long enough the first time."

"I waited over a year for you to ask me out. What's a few more months?" Kelsey asked.

"You have a point," Tyler sighed, and continued. "Honestly, Kelsey, I wasn't sure what to do. I didn't realize what was going on until we got to Port Townsend and you told me about LTO Holdings buying your parents' building. It was only there that I put it all together. I didn't have time to think, I just needed to stop the bleeding. So I told Lisa I would break up with you if she left you alone."

"But now of course, the deal's off," Kelsey said.

"Nothing will happen," Tyler replied, squeezing her hand.

"How can you be sure?" Kelsey asked.

"Because Princess, I have a plan."

Tyler rang the bell when they got to Ryan and Jess's condo. He grinned mischievously.

"I told Ryan I was coming over with my new girlfriend. Jessica has barely spoken to me in months." Kelsey knew that Jess was still furious about Tyler breaking up with Kelsey, instead of fighting Lisa so they could stay together, and it was clear that Tyler knew as well.

The door opened, and Tyler put his finger to his lips. Ryan looked at Kelsey in delight.

"Well, hello Tyler," Ryan said brightly. "This must be your new girlfriend."

"This is. Meet Ryan," Tyler said loudly, as they walked in. A pan clanged loudly in the kitchen. Jessica stood at the sink, her back to the door.

"Lovely to meet you," Ryan said, kissing Kelsey on the cheek. "Jessica, come meet Tyler's new girlfriend."

Jessica's shoulders slumped. She turned around slowly. A look of surprise spread over her face.

"Kelsey?" Jessica shouted. She ran over and gave Kelsey a big hug.

"You're back together? Since when?"

"Last night," Kelsey said, as Ryan closed the door.

Jessica frowned at Tyler and punched him hard in the arm.

"It took you long enough," she scolded him.

"You're speaking to me again," Tyler said, rubbing his arm where she had punched him.

"Perhaps," Jessica replied. She looked at Kelsey's hand, then took it into her own. "You're engaged?" she said in disbelief.

Ryan looked at Tyler. "Really, bro?" he asked delightedly.

"We are," Tyler said.

"You need to think about this," Jessica said to Kelsey, glaring at Tyler.

"No, she doesn't," Tyler replied.

"You think Lisa's going to accept Kelsey?" Jessica asked.

"I'm sure of it," Tyler said confidently.

"You're delusional," Jessica snapped.

"Don't worry about it," Kelsey said to Jessica.

"I'm going to do nothing but worry," Jessica replied.

"We didn't come over to talk about Lisa," Tyler commented as he handed Ryan the manila envelope.

"Then why are you here?" Jessica asked sassily.

"To eat," Tyler replied matter-of-factly.

"Brunch is almost ready," Ryan said.

"Jess? Can I talk to you for a minute?" Tyler asked. Jessica frowned a little but nodded.

"I'll help you in the kitchen, Ryan." Kelsey said as Tyler and Jessica walked over to the windows. Ryan glanced over in concern at Tyler, but said nothing. He placed the envelope on the top of the bar. Kelsey walked into the kitchen and washed her hands. Then she picked up a knife and began cutting the fruit that was sitting out on a cutting board.

She and Ryan worked silently, but there was virtually no sound from Tyler and Jess either. Jessica stood, arms crossed as Tyler spoke quietly.

Kelsey looked at them a few times, and she saw Ryan look over a few as well, as the one-sided conversation went on. Suddenly, Kelsey heard Jess.

"OK," Jess said. Kelsey glanced over, and to her surprise, Jessica hugged Tyler.

Kelsey glanced at Ryan, who was eavesdropping too. He was smiling. Jessica and Tyler walked toward the other two, and it was clear that Jessica's fight with Tyler was over.

"So what's for brunch?" Tyler asked Ryan.

Ryan served brunch, then sat at the table next to Jessica.

"Happy birthday, Ryan," Tyler said, as he scooped up a serving of scrambled eggs and put them on Kelsey's plate.

"Yes, happy birthday," Kelsey said. "And happy first anniversary to both of you."

"Thank you," Ryan said. He looked at Jessica mischievously. "I got the best gift ever last night."

Tyler rolled his eyes and Ryan grinned. "Jessica's pregnant," he said.

"Congratulations," Tyler said.

"Thank you," Jessica beamed.

Kelsey gave her a hug. "How many weeks?" Kelsey asked.

"Around eight. I've been hiding it from Ryan, but it was getting difficult," Jessica replied.

"She's spent weeks moaning about getting fat," Ryan said. "I didn't have a clue."

Jessica kissed him on the cheek. "I haven't gone to the doctor yet," Jessica said. "I didn't want Ryan to read about it in the press."

"We'll go tomorrow," Ryan added. He gently rubbed her tummy. "Make sure things are OK."

"No morning sickness?" Kelsey asked.

"A little, but not as bad as Kim," Jessica replied. "I've been lucky."

"Not as lucky as me," Ryan commented. Jessica ran her hand against Ryan's chin, and he looked at her lovingly.

Jessica smiled at Kelsey. "I guess we'll have to get a bigger place. So many memories here, though."

Kelsey nodded.

"But we can sell it and use the proceeds for a down payment on the next one," Jessica continued. Kelsey thought that Bob would probably be thrilled to buy a new house for his grandchild-to-be, but she didn't say anything.

Tyler looked from Ryan to Jessica, then back to Ryan.

"You didn't tell her," he said to Ryan. Tyler lifted his fork and took a bite of eggs. Ryan looked at Tyler with his bright blue eyes, as Jessica turned to Ryan.

"Tell me what?" she asked.

"Tyler," Ryan said.

"You were supposed to tell her right after Christmas."

"I hadn't gotten around to it," Ryan said.

"One sentence? Really?" Tyler said in annoyance.

"You haven't told Kelsey," Ryan retorted.

"I haven't seen Kelsey," Tyler replied irritably.

170

"Told us what?" Kelsey asked.

Tyler sighed. Ryan took Jessica's hand gently.

"We can't sell the condo," Ryan said.

"Why?" Jessica said.

"Because I've mortgaged it," Ryan said.

Jessica dropped his hand. "You did what?" she said. "Ryan, the condo is worth over four million dollars. Why in the world would you mortgage it?"

"Because Tyler needed the money," Ryan said simply.

Kelsey and Jessica both turned and looked at Tyler.

"Tyler, what's going on?" Kelsey said.

"Why do you need four million dollars?" Jessica asked.

Tyler took a bite of his toast and chewed it thoughtfully as the girls waited for him to speak. He swallowed, then said,

"Because I'm about to launch a proxy fight against Tactec."

"You're going to do what?" Jessica shouted.

Kelsey looked at Tyler in disbelief. She was no expert in corporate law, but she knew what a proxy fight was. They all did. Tyler was going to try to put his own people on the board of Tactec, which would give him more control over the direction of the company.

Kelsey struggled to think. "Tyler, you're really going to fight your mother over control of her board?" she finally asked. Jessica sat in her seat, her head shaking from side to side.

"Yes," Tyler said unconcernedly.

"And you think you're going to win?" Jessica asked.

"No," Tyler replied.

"Then why are you doing this? With Ryan's money?" Jessica asked.

"He'll get it back," Tyler said.

"Again, why are you doing this?" Jessica asked.

"I have my reasons," Tyler replied.

"Are you trying to replace the entire board?" Kelsey asked. Tactec's board had eight members. If Tyler managed to replace a majority, he could potentially oust Lisa as CEO.

"No. Only three of the members," Tyler said.

"Why only three? What will that do?" Jessica asked.

"It will make the board infinitely better," Tyler replied.

"I can't believe you're doing this," Jessica said. "She's your mother."

"That's why I'm doing it. That trio is going to drag the company into the ground. And Lisa's going to let them," Tyler said.

"And you're going to help Tyler?" Jessica asked Ryan. He nodded.

"I am," Ryan replied.

Jessica surveyed him. "Fine. It's your condo. But the baby and I aren't sleeping in a cardboard box when Tyler loses."

Ryan smiled at her. "You aren't mad?" he asked.

"Of course I'm mad," Jessica said. "But I knew you were insane when I met you."

Ryan gave her a hug. Tyler glanced at Kelsey, who bit her lip, but asked her question anyway.

"Is this what you've been working on at work for the past few months?" Kelsey asked.

"Yes," Tyler replied.

"So Bill's helping you?"

"Correct."

Kelsey wasn't sure what to think of this. Bill Simon had sued Tactec on behalf of clients numerous times in his career. But Bill Simon also wasn't in the habit of taking on cases he didn't think he could win. And of course Bill and Tyler weren't the best of friends.

"OK," Kelsey said.

"OK?" Tyler asked, looking at Kelsey with concern.

"Like Jessica said, I knew you were insane when I met you," Kelsey replied. Tyler smiled at her delightedly, and Kelsey couldn't help but smile back. "So what happens now?"

"I still have a lot of work to do," Tyler said. "But we'll initiate the proxy fight on February 15th."

"So Lisa will be screaming at you on the 16th," Jessica said.

"I don't think she'll wait that long," Tyler replied.

"It's your head," Jessica said. "And yours too," she said to Ryan.

"I know," Ryan said.

"But I asked Ryan so nicely," Tyler teased.

Ryan laughed. "It's the least I can do. I owe you one," he said.

"One?" Tyler asked.

Ryan grinned. "A few."

"Four million dollars should cover it," Jessica said.

"Not even close," Tyler replied, glancing at Ryan.

The conversation moved to the pregnancy and as they sat chatting with Ryan and Jess over potential baby names, and eating the delicious brunch, Kelsey found her mind wandering.

A proxy fight was a serious matter. Tyler was going to ask all of the shareholders of Tactec to vote to replace three of the members of the board, over the likely protests of Lisa Olsen. Tyler seemed completely unconcerned, but Kelsey wondered if this would be the last straw in Tyler's relationship with his mother.

She and Tyler held hands as they headed back across First Avenue after brunch. Tyler carried the large bag of clothing that Jessica had brought back for Kelsey from L.A.

"Are you sure about this?" Kelsey asked. "About starting a fight with your mother's company?"

Tyler was quiet for a moment, then he answered.

"Tyler, Lisa Olsen's son, can't marry you. But Tyler Olsen can."

At first, Kelsey wasn't sure what he meant. But instead of speaking, Kelsey surveyed Tyler's brown eyes thoughtfully. She thought back to everything that Tyler had said, everything that she had heard about Tyler and his relationship with Lisa.

Now she understood. This was Tyler's way of becoming Tyler Olsen.

The Tyler Olsen who wasn't just Lisa Olsen's son, but his own man. Whether he failed or not, after this, although others might think of him as just Lisa's son, Tyler never would think of himself that way again. This was his way of liberating himself.

"I see," Kelsey said.

"Do you?" Tyler asked. "Are you sure?"

"I do. I support you, Tyler Olsen," Kelsey said. "And I always will."

"Thank you. Mrs. Tyler Olsen-to-be," Tyler said with a smile.

Kelsey leaned against Tyler's arm. "You don't have to do this for me," she said.

"I'm not doing this for you," Tyler replied. Kelsey nodded. In her heart, she knew that he wasn't. All of his life, Tyler had been Lisa Olsen's son. Even at Simon and Associates, at least three times a week, when Bill was angry with Tyler, he would remind Tyler that he had another job, with

Lisa Olsen. On the other hand, Kelsey wasn't sure that Bill Simon knew she had parents.

Tyler had always lived in the shadow of his mother's success. No wonder he wanted to have a success of his own. But in Kelsey's view, and perhaps in Tyler's as well, it was a shame that he had to attack her company in order to get what he thought he wanted.

After a blissful Sunday afternoon of cuddling with Tyler, Kelsey took a deep breath and called her father.

"Hi, Kelsey," he said.

"Hi, Dad. Tyler asked me to marry him," Kelsey said.

"Did you say yes?" her father asked. He was clearly not surprised.

"I did," Kelsey said.

"Congratulations," her father said, and Kelsey was comforted by the happiness in his voice. "Do you want me to break the news to your mother?"

"That would be good," Kelsey admitted.

"I can do that for you."

"Thank you," Kelsey said. "Tyler said that he asked for your permission."

"He did. Before you left home."

"Which is how you knew about the fireworks," Kelsey said.

"Guilty," her father said.

"That was very sweet," Kelsey said. She was pleased that her father got along with Tyler. That was one less hurdle that they would have to cross.

"I'm happy for the two of you," Dan North said, and Kelsey could hear the new emotion in his voice.

"But concerned."

"You're my baby girl," he said unapologetically.

"OK, Dad."

"Kelsey, I don't want anything else to happen to you. Tyler has said that he's going to do everything in his power to make sure that you're safe, but if you ever feel like there's a problem, you need to tell me right away."

"I will," Kelsey promised.

"All right, then I'll try not to worry. I'll let your grandmother know, too."

"Thanks."

"Are you going to wear her dress?" Dan North teased.

"No," Kelsey said.

Her father laughed. "I won't tell her that," he said.

"That's probably for the best," Kelsey said.

"Take care of yourself, Kelsey."

"I will."

"I love you."

"I love you, Dad," Kelsey said, and they disconnected.

"Kelsey, can you join me?" Tyler asked as he stuck his head into her office on January 2nd. "I need to ask Simon something."

"OK," Kelsey said. She stood up, smoothed her dress, and walked over to Tyler. They walked through the virtually empty office. It was 7 a.m., and Tyler had asked Kelsey to come in early. They walked down the hall, hand in hand at the office for the first time in a very long time.

Bill Simon was sitting behind his desk.

"Can we come in?" Tyler asked.

"Sure," Simon said. He glanced at their clasped hands, but said nothing.

"I'd like permission to fire Ingrid," Tyler said without preamble.

Kelsey looked at him in surprise. So did Simon.

"Why? Ingrid's very capable. Do you just want me to transfer her to someone else?" Simon said to Tyler.

"Ingrid is my mother's spy," Tyler said.

"What?" Simon said, in shock. Kelsey's eyes widened.

"She was sent here to spy on me," Tyler explained patiently. "It's no longer useful for me to allow my mother to keep tabs on me, so I'd like to get rid of Ingrid."

Simon looked at Tyler thoughtfully. "Are you sure she's your mother's spy?" he asked.

"Positive," Tyler replied.

"I'd like to be there when you do it," Simon said.

178

"I'll let you know when she gets in," Tyler said brightly.

He gently led Kelsey out of the office, and took her hand and kissed it.

Kelsey looked at him and asked, "What is she supposed to report on?"

"You, I imagine," Tyler said. "Lisa probably wants to make sure that we aren't back together."

Kelsey immediately began to think about the questions that Ingrid had asked her, her interest in her relationship with Tyler, and everything else over the past few months.

"How long have you known?" Kelsey asked him.

"That Ingrid was spying on me? The week after I hired her," Tyler replied.

"Then why did you let her stay?" Kelsey asked in surprise.

"It gave Lisa false comfort. But now I have you back. I want to tell my mother personally," Tyler said.

Two hours later, Kelsey watched as Ingrid, clad in a bright blue coat, went past her office and walked down the hall. A few minutes later, Bill Simon strode briskly in front of Kelsey's office door.

"Come on," he said to Kelsey. She stood, and followed him.

They walked to Tyler's office. He looked up when they came in.

"Sit, I'll get her," Tyler said. Simon and Kelsey sat in the client chairs as Tyler stood up and walked over to his door. He stuck his head out.

"Ingrid, can you come in please?" he said brightly. A moment later,

Ingrid walked into the room, carrying a tablet.

"Close the door," Tyler said pleasantly to her. Ingrid did so. She glanced at Simon and Kelsey.

"I'll keep this brief. You're fired. Please tell my mother not to send over any more spies when you report to her."

Ingrid opened her mouth. Kelsey assumed she was about to defend herself and deny Tyler's accusation. Seeing the look on Tyler's face, Ingrid closed her mouth and nodded.

"OK," she said simply.

Simon looked at Ingrid harshly. "Building security is at your desk. Make sure that you don't take anything that doesn't belong to you. You have five minutes."

Ingrid nodded.

"Goodbye, Ingrid," Tyler said pleasantly.

"Goodbye, Mr. Olsen," Ingrid said, and she left. Simon followed her out.

Tyler smiled at Kelsey.

"Well, that was fun." He sighed. "But now I need a new secretary."

"You can't share mine," Kelsey teased.

"We're back together. What's yours is mine," Tyler replied.

"You wish," Kelsey replied.

"I do," Tyler grinned. "But it will be."

Kelsey and Tyler's phones buzzed within seconds of each other when they were eating lunch. They both looked at their messages, then at each other, then they exchanged phones.

Tyler's message from Ryan read: *Twins!*

Kelsey's message from Jessica read: *Twins?*

Tyler laughed as he handed Kelsey's phone back to her. "Poor Jess. On the other hand, she'll be much closer to reaching Ryan's goal of five kids."

At 2 p.m., Kelsey headed to an all-office meeting. As she passed by, she saw Millie lock the front door. Kelsey walked into the conference room where everyone except Tyler, Millie, and Bill were already sitting.

"What's going on?" asked Amie. Kelsey shrugged. The last three people came into the conference room and sat down. Everyone looked at Bill expectantly.

He looked around the table, and Kelsey noticed he looked quite serious.

"Thank you all for taking the time to be here. I have an announcement that will affect all of us." He paused for a moment. Kelsey could feel the slight anxiety in the room, but she also noticed that Tyler seemed completely unconcerned.

Bill continued. "We have a new client, who we will be representing in a proxy battle against Tactec. His name is Tyler Olsen."

Jaws dropped around the table, but everyone remained silent.

"Tyler has been working on this project for a while. We plan on notifying Tactec in mid-February. Their annual meeting is the first week of April. Part of the reason I have requested this meeting is to remind everyone of their legal requirement to keep their client's confidences, and of course, this requirement also applies to Tyler's project."

There were silent nods around the room.

"Tyler, there was something else you wanted to announce?" Bill asked.

"There is," Tyler said. "Kelsey and I are engaged."

The room went from silent to cries of delight.

"Congratulations!" Millie said happily, giving Kelsey a side hug.

"Wow," Tori said.

"Um," Devin commented. He was clearly surprised.

"Just friends," Jake whispered to Kelsey. She grinned and he smiled back.

A few minutes later, the entire office was eating cake. Jake had switched seats with Tyler, who was now eating cake off Kelsey's fork.

"You've been going out with Tyler?" Tori asked in amazement.

"You should leave your office occasionally, Tori," Marie commented.

"If I left my office, Tyler would have to do my work, and wouldn't have had time to seduce Kelsey," Tori retorted. Kelsey blushed and Tyler grinned.

"So when are you getting married?" Millie asked between bites of cake. Kelsey glanced at Tyler. They hadn't discussed a time.

"This weekend?" Tyler asked hopefully.

"This summer," Kelsey said definitively. She fed Tyler another bite of cake, but he didn't look happy.

"So how did you figure out that Ingrid was spying on you?" Kelsey asked him as he walked her home that evening.

"I'm thinking I shouldn't tell you," he commented.

Kelsey looked at Tyler, who looked sheepish.

"I'm thinking you should," Kelsey said, a bit sharply. *What was Tyler hiding?*

"Do you love me?" Tyler asked.

"Yes."

"Do you trust me?" he asked.

"What did you do?" Kelsey demanded.

"I made a pass at her," Tyler said.

"You did what?" Kelsey said. She stopped on the sidewalk and dropped his hand.

"I knew I shouldn't have told you," Tyler said, grinning.

"OK, with that look, there's more to this story," Kelsey said, taking his hand again.

"There is," Tyler said.

"Fine, I trust you, Mr. Olsen. Now tell me why you made a pass at your pretty, blonde secretary," Kelsey said. "This better be good," she added.

"I had my doubts about Ingrid when I hired her. She's a little too perfect.

It's like a computer program came up with her. But then Ryan told me that Jess had reported that Ingrid was interested in me. Of course I knew where Jess had gotten that information from."

"Ingrid asked me about you," Kelsey confirmed.

"I thought that was interesting. Week one, and Ingrid's already asking around about my dating status. So it's one of two things. Love at first sight, or she's snooping around."

"You're a billionaire. Everyone knows that," Kelsey said.

"So it must be love?" Tyler asked.

Kelsey grinned. "Exactly."

"I thought so too. I thought I'd test that theory."

"Why?"

"Kelsey, I needed a secretary, not a new girlfriend. If she was going to spend office hours trying to get me into bed, I was going to fire her right away. So I invited her to lunch."

"And?" Kelsey asked.

Tyler cleared his throat.

"Let's just say I suggested that significant bonuses could come her way if she was interested in taking them," he said. Kelsey's mouth dropped open.

"But she turned me down flat. She was exceedingly polite, but she said that she wanted me to understand that she simply wanted a professional relationship with me, and that she hoped I would keep her as my secretary, because she enjoyed working with me."

"I told her that was very happy having her as my secretary and that she could expect a purely professional relationship from here on," Tyler concluded.

"So you decided that she was a spy because she wouldn't sleep with you? How arrogant is that?"

"You're forgetting something, Miss North. Didn't Ingrid tell you that she was interested in me?"

Kelsey thought. "Yes," she said.

"So why would she turn me down?" Tyler asked. "That doesn't make sense. She'll tell a perfect stranger that she's interested in me, then when I offer myself to her, she says no?"

"OK, that is weird," Kelsey agreed.

"So I decided that she was probably snooping."

"Did you follow her? Hire a detective?" Kelsey teased.

"I called Zach. He sat in the Tactec lobby across the street on an afternoon when I told Ingrid she could leave early, and which coincidently was Lisa's day in Seattle."

"You're kidding."

"Zach doesn't have anything better to do."

"No, I mean, how did you know she'd go to your mother's office?" Kelsey asked.

"Oh, that's easy. I told Ingrid I had a date. I knew she'd want to report that."

"Did you?"

"Of course not," Tyler said, dismissively.

"Why wouldn't she just call your mother?"

"She could have, but I took the risk. Like I said, Zach doesn't have anything better to do."

As they reached Kelsey's door, Tyler kissed her hand.

"We can't get married until this summer?" he asked. "I thought we could drive to Port Townsend one weekend. You said you wanted to get married in front of your family and friends."

"What about yours?" Kelsey asked.

"My what?" Tyler replied.

"Your family," Kelsey replied.

"Kelsey, I'm about to start a proxy fight against my mother."

"Tyler, you need to have your family there. At least one of your parents."

Tyler looked doubtful.

"You have to at least try," Kelsey conceded.

"OK, but then we have to wait to announce our engagement. I don't want Lisa coming after you again."

"Fine." She had told her parents, and that was enough for now.

"I really have to wait until this summer?" Tyler asked. They had reached Kelsey's apartment door, and Kelsey looked up into his sexy brown eyes.

"You do."

Tyler pulled Kelsey close, and kissed her on the lips.

"Fine," he replied. "OK, Princess. If you say so."

"I do," Kelsey teased. She gave Tyler a gentle kiss, then walked into her apartment.

On Thursday evening, Kelsey was sitting at her desk, working on a client letter, when Tyler looked in.

"Dinner?" he asked.

Kelsey looked up at him in surprise. "What are you doing here? I expected Zach to call," she replied.

"Oh, right, you haven't been here. I'm done with my treatment," Tyler said, walking over and giving her a gentle kiss.

"You are?" Kelsey asked.

Tyler nodded. "Since mid-December," he replied, as he sat in one of the client chairs.

Kelsey thought about what this meant. She knew that Tyler had been steadily gaining control of his eating disorder ever since he had started treatment, but she didn't know enough about his treatment to know what was considered success.

"So you're OK now?" Kelsey asked.

"My doctor thinks that it's under control," Tyler replied.

"And you?"

"I think I know what triggers it, and what signs to look for to make sure it doesn't get out of control again. Plus, I'll have a live-in eating coach soon."

Kelsey smiled at him.

"I suppose you will," she replied.

On Saturday after work, Kelsey and Tyler sat in her apartment, cuddling on the sofa again, Tyler nuzzled her happily.

"I've missed this," he said.

"What?"

"Just holding you," Tyler replied.

"Me, too," Kelsey agreed. While they were used to talking together, touching had been the missing piece in their relationship, and Kelsey realized just how much she missed being caressed by Tyler. As she lay in his arms, she felt wonderful. "I'm so happy today," she said peacefully.

"So am I," Tyler agreed. They sat quietly together, until Kelsey had a question. It was one that had been plaguing her every since she had found about the proxy fight, and she decided that she might as well ask.

"Tyler, why are you starting a proxy fight?"

"Well, if I were Ryan, I would say because I can. But the real reason is that thanks to my mother and Bob's hard work, I'm a billionaire, and I intend to remain one. I'm not going to let Lisa run the company into the ground. Tactec won't last another ten years without different leadership."

"But you're not going to try to force your mother out?" Kelsey asked.

"No. Frankly, I'm not confident of getting any of my own people on the board of directors this time. I'm considering this a shot across the bow, a wake-up call."

"The media is going to crucify you," Kelsey commented.

Tyler laughed. "If I've learned anything from Lisa and Ryan, it's to ignore the media."

"What happened to you?" Kelsey asked him thoughtfully.

"What do you mean?"

"You've changed."

"I lost you. I'm not going to let it happen again. My whole life I've played defense against Lisa Olsen and her ambitions. It's my turn to attack. *Audentes fortuna juvat.* Fortune favors the bold."

Kelsey leaned her head into Tyler and he stroked her hair. She loved Tyler, and she trusted him. But she was afraid for him. What would this do to his relationship with his mother? What did it mean for their relationship together? Kelsey didn't know.

"Why didn't you tell me that you were doing this?" Kelsey asked Tyler.

Tyler was silent for a moment. Kelsey knew he was thinking.

"I didn't want to worry you," Tyler finally said.

"I've done nothing but worry," Kelsey admitted.

"Why?" Tyler asked, puzzled.

"Because I didn't know what you were doing."

"And that worried you?" Tyler asked. He stroked her hair again. "Is that why you asked me and Zach so many questions?"

"Yeah," Kelsey said.

Tyler was silent again. "I thought I was protecting you," he finally said.

"I'd rather know what's going on," Kelsey replied.

"I'm sorry," Tyler said. "I won't have secrets from you any more, Kelsey."

"Tyler, I didn't mean that. You don't have to tell me everything. Just the important things."

"OK, I can do that. I don't want my Princess to worry about anything."

"I'm not sure you can control that," Kelsey commented wryly.

"I'm going to try," Tyler said, bending down and kissing her forehead.

On Sunday, Kelsey joined Tyler, Zach, Brandon, Jess, and Ryan in the large conference room at Simon and Associates. Bill Simon was in his office, which didn't come as a complete surprise to Kelsey. She had long suspected that he worked every day, including the Sundays that his associates took off. There always seemed to be lots of new assignments waiting in the office on Monday morning.

All of their phones sat in the middle of the table, untouched. Tyler was writing on a white legal pad in his neat handwriting with one of the black ballpoint pens that could be found around the office. Their meeting had just begun.

"Ryan," Tyler said.

"Nothing," Ryan replied. "No one's said anything to me."

"Good," Tyler said, with a smile on his face. "Eve said the money's safely in my client account."

Kelsey and Jess glanced at each other. This was the first time that they had been invited to the boys' meeting, and they would need to pay attention to catch up. Kelsey assumed that Tyler was referring to the money that Ryan had received from mortgaging his condo. Simon had probably set up a client account for the money, and the expenses for the proxy fight would be paid out of the account.

"Zach."

"Medina is nice and quiet, although Lisa's not happy about you skipping the Tactec party and Christmas."

"She'll get over it," Tyler said dismissively. "Brandon."

"I'm on slide 35," Brandon said.

"That's all?" Zach said to him.

"I have a lot of work at work," Brandon replied.

"Dude, the website's ready to go," Zach said.

"We have time," Brandon said.

"Time for what?" Jessica asked. "Kelsey and I have no idea what you're talking about."

Tyler glanced at Jessica.

"In a proxy fight, you have to lay out a case as to why the shareholders should vote for your slate of candidates," Tyler explained. "Zach has built a website which will allow shareholders to see our presentation, and Brandon is creating the actual presentation."

"It's going to be over 35 slides?" Kelsey asked.

"I expect it to be about 250," Tyler replied. "There's a lot to say."

"Who's going to go through 250 slides?" Jessica asked in disbelief.

"You'd be surprised," Zach replied. Kelsey supposed that as a venture capitalist who had probably seen a lot of presentations, Zach would know.

"We're laying out a case for the disruption of a multi-billion dollar company. The shareholders are going to want to know why," Brandon said.

Jessica nodded. "I'll help you." she said to Brandon. Everyone looked at Jess in surprise.

"Jess, you're pregnant," Ryan said, a bit of worry in his voice.

"So? I don't think the babies will mind if I sit and help make a Powerpoint presentation. Anyway, maybe I'll understand what's going on better," Jessica said.

"That would be great, Jess," Tyler said. "Please just make sure that you don't use any computer from or at Tactec."

Jessica nodded.

"I'll forward the files to Ryan tonight," Brandon said.

"OK," Jessica said.

"Kelsey," Tyler said.

"Yes?" Kelsey said, startled. She wasn't expecting to be called on. The only thing that she was doing was holding the key to the money Tyler had put in her safe deposit box.

Tyler winked at her. "Just making sure that you're listening," he teased.

Kelsey frowned. "My ears are wide open, Mr. Olsen," she replied.

"Good." Tyler grinned. "OK, Bill and I have set out the timetable. February 15th is our date, so we don't have a lot of time. I talk to Rebecca Jones tomorrow."

"And what happens when she turns you down?" Brandon asked.

"Then I'm probably going to have to find someone out-of-state. I'm going to have to go to New York in March anyway, so I'll look there if I need to."

"Why will you have to go to New York?" Jessica asked.

"I'm going to have to make some in-person presentations, plus I'll need to talk to the media," Tyler replied. "I'll probably need to go to San Francisco as well."

"Yeah, this is what I wanted to do with my spring," Zach said.

"What are you complaining about?" Brandon asked.

"Dude, I'm dead as soon as Tyler announces this. There's no way my mother is going to believe that I wasn't helping him," Zach commented.

"Are you kidding me?" Brandon said. "My father will probably be assigned to take Tyler down. You know Lisa's going to bring out the artillery. She hates being challenged."

Kelsey and Jessica looked at each other again. The boys seemed pretty calm, but Kelsey knew that both she and Jess were thinking about Lisa Olsen's rage. Both of them had experienced it, and who knew how Lisa would react to an attack on her company?

"We'll be fine," Tyler said comfortingly. "The proxy fight is only six weeks, then it's over."

"The longest six weeks of our lives," Zach replied.

Kelsey was nervous as they waited for Bill Simon to arrive with the guest for their 6 p.m. meeting. Although legal counsel was important in a proxy fight, the most critical component was the public relations team. It was important to be able to tell your story to the media, as they were your most important link to what the shareholders thought of your offering.

Because of this, Tyler had explained to her that he felt that it was vital that Rebecca Jones represent him. Ms. Jones had developed a national reputation for her ability to give her clients the best forums to reach their desired targets through the media. Ms. Jones was the consultant of choice for anyone in a public relations crisis, and beginning a proxy fight against your mother's company surely qualified. Tyler knew that he would need all of the help he could get.

Bill Simon walked into the conference room, followed by an attractive African-American woman in a black suit. She strode confidently into the room and reached out her hand to Tyler, who had stood when she walked in.

"Mr. Olsen," she said, shaking his hand.

"It's nice to meet you, Ms. Jones. This is my fiancee, Kelsey North," Tyler replied.

Despite her nerves, Kelsey liked being called Tyler's fiancee and she smiled a tiny bit.

"Ms. North," Ms. Jones said, shaking Kelsey's hand.

"Kelsey will be representing Tyler," Bill Simon said. Kelsey looked at Bill in surprise, and he winked at her.

"I see," Ms. Jones said, sitting down in a chair. She fixed Tyler with a serious look. "Mr. Olsen, I'll be honest with you, I wouldn't be here if Bill hadn't called me personally and told me that his office was representing you."

"I understand," Tyler replied. "It's been difficult to have people take me seriously."

Ms. Jones nodded thoughtfully. "I can believe that. So this isn't a mommy issue that you need to discuss with a therapist?"

"The only issue that I have is that Tactec's stock price is too low," Tyler replied.

"And you've decided to attack your mother's company in the most public of ways because why?"

"Because after trying numerous other avenues, I decided to go with the option of last resort."

"Why now?"

"The stock is languishing, and frankly, I want it to go up before I can start diversifying the shares in my trust."

"So this is about money?"

"Of course."

"Mr. Olsen, the stock hasn't dropped significantly, and it's likely to go up over the next few years," Ms. Jones countered.

Tyler shook his head.

"Not with these board members. If the problem isn't contained now, Tactec is going to continue its downward slide," Tyler replied.

"And to counter that, you're going to attack your mother."

"No, this has nothing to do with my mother. This is about the board members. My mother is doing an excellent job with the board that she has," Tyler replied.

Ms. Jones lifted an eyebrow. "So you aren't going to criticize the CEO?"

"No, I'm not," Tyler replied.

"You agree with this, Bill? That this isn't personal?"

"I wouldn't have called you otherwise," Bill Simon said. "Tyler is right, there is a significant problem with Tactec's board, and unfortunately for the shareholders of Tactec, there aren't a lot of people willing to go head-to-head with Lisa Olsen over her choices. If Tyler wants to, I've decided to help him."

"Yeah, but you don't like Tactec," Ms. Jones replied, referring to his unwillingness to do work for the company.

"It's not that I don't like the company," Bill Simon said. "But I think Tyler has made a good case for intervening this time."

"Can you win?" Ms. Jones asked Tyler. Kelsey bit her lip. Rebecca Jones was nothing if not direct.

"I don't think so," Tyler replied. "I'm not sure I'm going to find the votes."

"Then why are you doing this?"

"Because I hope that if I can make my case now, the shareholders will start to consider voting for better board members in the following annual meeting."

"Tactec holds annual meetings for their directors?" Ms. Jones asked.

"Yes, since 2008, shareholders vote for every member of the board. It's a one-year term," Tyler replied.

"When do you want to begin?"

"Mid-February. Five weeks from now."

"When's the annual meeting?"

"Early April," Tyler replied.

"That's about the right amount of time. Why aren't you getting someone else to front the battle? Why you?" Ms. Jones asked.

"I figure that my story is so interesting, that the media will do most of my work for me," Tyler replied.

"That it is. Son breaks his mother's heart," Ms. Jones said. But Tyler didn't react.

Ms. Jones sat quietly for a moment, thinking. "You know my fee?" Ms. Jones said to Tyler.

Tyler smiled, and Kelsey breathed a sigh of relief. If they were talking money, Ms. Jones had decided to take Tyler on.

"I do," Tyler replied.

"And you have the money?"

"I do," Tyler repeated.

"Is it your mother's?"

"No," Tyler replied. Kelsey smiled to herself. Thanks to Tyler's deal with Ryan, it was Bob's money that Tyler was using. She wondered how Bob would feel about that.

Ms. Jones looked at Tyler's eyes. "Fine, we'll do this. But you're going to do what I ask you to do. You're a baby, and the media is going to treat you like one. So we're going to spend as much time as possible countering that."

"OK," Tyler said. Ms. Jones stood up.

"My secretary will be in touch with you tomorrow. Class begins next week," she said.

"Thank you," Tyler said. He and Bill stood.

Ms. Jones looked at Tyler carefully. "I mean it, Mr. Olsen. You'd better not screw this up."

"I won't," Tyler replied. Ms. Jones turned and Bill escorted her out of the room.

Tyler sat heavily in a chair. He looked at Kelsey.

"Are you ready?" he asked.

"No," Kelsey said honestly.

"Me neither," Tyler said, taking her hand. They sat silently until Bill returned alone.

"Well done," Bill said, sitting back down. "I never thought she'd take you on."

"Did she say why she did?" Tyler asked.

Bill smiled. "Knowing Becks, she's hoping to talk you out of it."

"Good luck with that," Tyler commented.

"So here's how the next few weeks are going to go. Tyler, you're going to be on half-time for me. Kelsey, I want you to attend all of the meetings concerning the proxy vote, including those with Rebecca. Make sure you bill all of your time," Bill Simon said, pointedly.

"I'm expecting a discount," Tyler said.

"You won't be getting one," Bill Simon said.

"Bill, why do I need to be in the meetings?" Kelsey asked.

"You're going to be Tyler's counsel, you're going to need to know what's going on," Bill said.

"Bill, I'm an IP lawyer," Kelsey said.

"You're going to be Tyler's wife, so whatever dumb idea he comes up with, you're going to need to help him with," Bill commented.

"Thanks for the comfort, Bill," Tyler said.

"Tyler, I'm going to help you so you don't run yourself into the ground. But I never said this was a good idea," Bill said.

"When I win, you'll change your mind."

"You can't win this year, so I doubt it," Bill replied.

"Just think long-term," Tyler said brightly.

Tyler was in good spirits over the next few days, despite or perhaps because he was in the office all of the time. In fact, Kelsey suspected that after he walked her home late at night, that he returned to the office to work some more.

On Thursday night, Kelsey had a surprise when Zach and Tyler walked into her office at 7 p.m.

"Tyler said you missed me," Zach grinned.

Tyler rolled his eyes. "I didn't say that," Tyler replied.

"But I did." Kelsey teased

"See?" Zach said to Tyler.

"Whatever," Tyler replied.

"Anyway," Zach said, ignoring Tyler, "I told Tyler we should go out for dinner. Does that work for you?"

Kelsey glanced at her computer. "I still have about another hour of work," she admitted.

"Not everyone has nothing to do," Tyler said to Zach.

"I can wait for an hour," Zach said. "Anyway it's not like I have nothing to do. There's a new game on my phone."

Kelsey laughed as Tyler sighed.

An hour later, the trio was walking up South Weller Street.

"Where are we going?" Kelsey asked. She was holding Tyler's hand, and felt warm in the cold January air.

"A great restaurant," Zach said.

"If it's open," Tyler added.

"What do you mean?" Kelsey asked. It wasn't that late.

"They get closed by the health department all the time," Tyler said.

"Seriously? And we're eating there?" Kelsey asked.

"The food's great," Zach commented. "And you only live once," he added.

Kelsey warily sat down at the table by the window a few minutes later. The restaurant was nondescript, and there were several families happily sitting and enjoying their meals, so she supposed that whatever violations that the health department had found had been corrected. At least that was how she comforted herself.

Tyler and Zach discussed what to order as Kelsey looked out onto the quiet street. It was raining gently, and the street lights shone off the wet pavement.

"So how's engaged life?" Zach asked her, as the waitress took the menus and walked off.

"Fine," Kelsey said with a smile. Tyler winked at her.

"Tyler's ecstatic," Zach commented.

"That I am," Tyler said.

"So when are you getting married?" Zach asked Kelsey.

"This summer."

Zach looked at Tyler. "You were serious," he said.

"It's Kelsey's idea. We would be married already if I had anything to do with it."

"Why are you making him wait?"

"I want a real wedding," Kelsey said. "With family and friends. Including Tyler's parents."

Zach burst out in laughter. "Both of Tyler's parents? I'll be married before the two of you will if Tyler needs to talk to his parents," he said.

"That's what I told Kelsey, but she didn't believe me."

"Tyler will work things out."

"Tyler is smart, but he's not a miracle worker," Zach pointed out.

"I have faith in him," Kelsey said, and Tyler sighed.

"Speaking of insolvable problems, how's Medina?" Tyler asked Zach.

"That is a great question," Zach commented.

"Which is why I asked it."

"Patience. You'll like this. So the tree-hugger was at Lisa's..."

"The tree-hugger?" Kelsey asked.

"An ironic name for Lisa's current boyfriend," Tyler replied.

"I see," Kelsey said. Since he was the head of a timber company, she understood the irony. "Go on."

"OK, so he's at Lisa's for dinner, and he's complaining about how he wasn't invited to the Tactec party."

"It was a month ago," Tyler commented.

"He's still very upset," Zach replied. "So Lisa told him for the eightieth time that she never has a date at the Tactec event."

"Tim was there," Tyler commented.

"That was business," Zach said. "He was taking over the IP portfolio."

"I see. Lisa logic."

"Yeah, well, the tree-hugger didn't like it either. He complained that Lisa isn't serious about him."

"Of course she isn't," Tyler said.

"He doesn't seem to know that. So anyway, Lisa tells my mom that he's not going to last until Valentine's."

"I guess she doesn't want a gift," Tyler commented. "So who's next?"

Zach shrugged. "The reason I know all of this is because my mom was trying to get Dad to come up with some names over lunch."

"Your poor father," Tyler said.

"Actually, I don't think he minds. Lisa's considered quite the catch. Rich and hot."

"My mother's not hot," Tyler said.

"You say that because she's your mom," Zach said.

"You are so sick," Tyler said, and Zach laughed as the waitress brought over a plate of vegetables. Kelsey lifted her chopsticks and picked up a green vegetable. It was interesting what guys talked about with each other, she thought.

"So that's another one gone," Zach said, picking up his own chopsticks.

"I'd say she's going to run out of options, but there always seems to be another one just waiting for his opportunity," Tyler mused.

"Plus she could always go out-of-state," Zach commented.

"They would have to come to her. She's not flying anywhere for anybody."

"Except for Rick Burton. He thinks she's hot too," Zach said deadpan.

Tyler laughed. "And she's already traveling out-of-state, thanks to him and his destruction of her acquisition. A match made in heaven."

"She should have listened to you," Zach said.

"Of course she should have. But of course she didn't," Tyler replied.

Kelsey picked up another vegetable, and offered it to Tyler, who ate it.

"I forgot how annoying the two of you are," Zach commented, eating his own vegetables.

"You can go back to the Eastside," Tyler pointed out.

"I'm here to see Miss North," Zach replied. "Who is very quiet tonight."

"Just listening," Kelsey replied.

"My mother's personal life is riveting," Tyler said sarcastically. "What else is happening in Medina?"

"Brandon's dad is working out of the Seattle office now," Zach said.

"That's interesting news. Since when?"

"The first of the year. You haven't talked to Brandon?"

"Not about his father. What does Sydney think?"

"You can imagine."

"I certainly can," Tyler said. Kelsey could too. Sydney, the Chief Legal Officer of Tactec, was no fan of attorney Richard Kinnon — who was also Lisa's friend — probably because she was concerned about losing her job. "Anything else?"

"Just the usual. Lisa's worried about you. She needs to go on vacation but can't be bothered. There's a half-dozen startups she wants to buy but doesn't have time. Nothing new."

"And you haven't found out anything else?"

"Not yet. Give me time."

"I don't have time. The letter goes out on the fifteenth."

"That's more than a month," Zach pointed out.

"That's not long at all," Tyler replied.

"Plenty of time," Zach said unconcernedly, taking another vegetable.

Tyler frowned, but Kelsey offered him another vegetable, and he seemed to brighten up. He ate it.

"I see Miss North is making sure you eat," Zach said.

"I need to be healthy if we're going to do this," Tyler replied.

"No, you don't. Because Lisa's going to kill you."

"Don't I know it," Tyler said, but he didn't seem overly concerned. Kelsey supposed that he was used to battling his mother, much like Kelsey was used to battling her own. It only seemed dramatic from the outside.

"I've been trying to figure out my alibi, but I'm not going to have one. Mom's going to be furious," Zach said thoughtfully.

"Sorry."

"It's not your fault," Zach said. "I mean, it is. But I understand."

"I appreciate your help," Tyler said. "But save yourself if you need to."

"No, it's OK," Zach said as the waitress brought over three bowls of rice and a giant bowl of seafood curry. Kelsey looked into the bowl, which was hot and bubbling, and smelled delicious. "I'm trying to schedule some meetings on the fifteenth, so I'll be out of the office. Maybe I'll fly down to Silicon Valley. Find some new investments."

"That sounds like a good idea," Tyler agreed. "Fly out the morning of the 15th, and stay there through the weekend. Lisa should be done shouting by then."

"That's what you think," Zach commented.

"I don't care. She brought all of this on herself," Tyler replied.

Zach glanced at Kelsey with his dark eyes.

"Our own little Helen of Troy," he said.

"Was this the face that launched a thousand ships?" Tyler quoted.

Kelsey looked at both of them. "What?" she asked.

"If you're marrying Tyler, you'll need to brush up on your Greek mythology," Zach said, picking up his spoon and dipping it into the curry.

"Wars were fought because Helen of Troy was so beautiful," Tyler said. Kelsey understood. She was at least part of the reason why Tyler was about to begin his own war.

Tyler spooned some curry into Kelsey's bowl.

"Thank you," Kelsey said, and she picked up her spoon and tasted it. She realized why the boys were willing to risk food poisoning. It was delicious.

Tyler had his own spoonful of curry. "Do you like it, Princess?" he asked.

Kelsey nodded. "It's great," she replied.

"Princess?" Zach said in amusement.

"Quiet," Tyler said.

"Maybe I don't want you two to be back together," Zach teased. "You've only been engaged for ten days. Imagine what you'll be like in ten years."

"I can't wait," Tyler said, looking at Kelsey with a sparkle in his eyes.

Kelsey sat on her living room floor late on Friday night, next to Tyler, who was lying on his stomach reading a book.

"Hungry?" Kelsey asked.

Tyler glanced up at her. Then his eyes returned to his book. "For you," he replied.

"Tyler Davis Olsen," Kelsey said with a sigh.

"Yes?"

"You're a pain," Kelsey said.

Tyler looked at her with a grin. "I'm your fiance, actually."

"And a pain."

"You want to sleep with me as much as I want to sleep with you," Tyler said matter-of-factly.

"That's what you think," Kelsey said dismissively.

"That's what I know," Tyler replied. "I know you missed me."

Kelsey paused before she spoke, because suddenly she felt a rush of emotion.

"I did," she said in almost a whisper.

Tyler turned and looked at her. "I didn't mean to make to make you sad, Princess," he said. He put his book aside, and sat up. Tyler gently put his arms around her.

Kelsey closed her eyes, to stop the tears that were beginning to pool in them. She leaned her head against his chest.

"Kelsey?" Tyler asked in concern. But Kelsey couldn't answer him. She had broken down in tears.

Kelsey couldn't stop crying. She felt like she was crying all of the tears that she had held in over the past eight months. She lay motionless in his arms as the tears rolled down her face.

Tyler held her tightly, and she sobbed.

A half-hour later, Tyler handed Kelsey a glass of water. She was sitting on the sofa and her tears had finally slowed. He brushed a lone tear off her cheek.

"Do you feel better?" he asked as Kelsey took a drink of water. She nodded, and looked at Tyler's concerned face.

"I'm OK," she said. Tyler stroked her face gently, took the glass of water out of her hand, and placed it on the coffee table. Then he wrapped his arms around her once more. He kissed her cheek.

"I didn't realize you were so devastated that we hadn't slept together," Tyler quipped. Kelsey hit him with a sofa pillow and sniffled. Tyler laughed, then he looked a bit more serious. "What happened? Are you sure that you're OK?"

Kelsey nodded and cuddled next to him. He held her tightly.

"Never again," he said softly. "I'm never going to be apart from you again."

Kelsey sat in Jessica's living room on Saturday afternoon. In front of them was a brand new Apple computer, which was displaying Tyler's Powerpoint presentation, slide by slide. Jessica looked at it thoughtfully, while at the same time yarn was moving quickly through her fingers as she knit a cotton baby hat. Kelsey marveled at the fact that Jessica could do both at once. Perhaps it was easier now that Jessica was no longer wearing her enormous engagement ring.

"What do you think of slide 74?" Jess asked, reaching out and pausing the slideshow. "I think the font could be a little bigger."

"I don't think it matters," Kelsey commented.

Jessica smiled at her. "You don't think anyone is really going to go through all of these slides, do you?"

"No," Kelsey admitted.

"Yeah, me neither," Jessica said. "But I said I'd work on it, so I am."

"It seems to be going well," Kelsey commented. "You're already on slide 125."

"I've been doing it after work," Jessica said. "And Ryan's been helping after we eat dinner."

"Are you OK with this?" Kelsey asked.

"OK with what?" Jessica asked.

"Everything. Tyler using Ryan's condo for his proxy fight. Tyler and me being back together again. Anything and everything that involves Tyler being back in your lives," Kelsey replied.

Jessica set the knitting on her lap. Her pregnancy was already beginning to show.

"I thought about that. I was angry with Tyler for so long. But when he walked in with you on New Year's Day, I realized that you were right. That Tyler loved you and that he was doing what he could to protect you and to eventually get you back. For a long time, I thought that you were deluding yourself about him, but I guess I was wrong, and you and Ryan were right," Jessica replied. She picked up the light green hat, and began knitting again.

"I've been wrong about a lot of things over the past year," Jessica continued. "I thought Tyler wasn't going to come back to you, I thought my mother was going to pick my father over me, I thought I wouldn't get pregnant before Ryan's deadline. I think I need to stop being so confident in my own judgment and listen to other people a little more."

"I see," Kelsey said.

"So, yeah, I'm OK with Tyler," Jessica said, as her fingers flew around the circular needles.

Kelsey had another question, but she felt that this one was a bit more delicate.

"Have you told your family that you're pregnant?" she asked.

Jessica set the knitting back down, and looked at Kelsey. She sighed.

"I did. I called Andrea and asked her to tell my mother."

"But?"

Jessica sighed once again. "My mother wants to be at the delivery."

Kelsey looked at Jessica in surprise.

"That's great," Kelsey said, but Jessica shook her head, and her auburn curls brushed her cheeks as she did so.

"I don't know how she's going to pull that one off without my father knowing. And I don't know how he's going to react if he finds out." Jessica picked up the knitting again, but this time, Kelsey thought that she was doing it to soothe her nerves.

"Did you tell her that?"

"She said that she wasn't going to miss the birth of her daughter's children, no matter what. So I wasn't sure what else to say."

"I'm sure it will work out," Kelsey said comfortingly.

"I hope so," Jessica said softly.

Ryan and Tyler arrived that evening to take the girls to dinner. Ryan gave his bride a kiss, while Kelsey delighted in getting a kiss from her fiance.

"How was your day?" Tyler asked her.

"Wonderful," Kelsey replied.

"Are you sure you don't want me to cook?" Ryan asked.

"Let's go out. We haven't been on a double date in a while," Tyler replied.

"It has been a long time," Ryan said, brushing Jessica's curls with his hand.

"I'm starving, so I hope you know where we're going," Jessica said to him.

"No," Ryan teased. Jessica frowned and Ryan kissed her again. "But Tyler does."

"So where are we going?" Jessica asked Tyler.

"You'll see," Tyler said with a smile.

"Shouldn't you be trying to save money?" Kelsey asked Tyler. "You do have a proxy battle to fight."

"I think I can afford to spend some money on my wife-to-be," Tyler replied.

"Some," Kelsey agreed. "But how much did you spend on this?"

"Enough," Tyler replied.

"You two are insane," Jessica said.

"That we are," Tyler replied.

"It is beautiful, though," Kelsey said, as she leaned against Tyler and looked out of the gigantic window of the yacht that they were standing on. Behind them a small staff was arranging the private dinner that Tyler had ordered for the two couples.

"Almost as nice as Bob's," Ryan said.

"We'll have dinner on his next time," Tyler commented. "I don't want the staff to be the one to tell him we're engaged," Tyler added, nuzzling Kelsey's ear.

"This is magical," Jessica said.

"We've been neglecting you," Ryan said. "We wanted to make it up to you."

"Before we neglect you some more," Tyler admitted.

"You have a lot to do. It's OK," Kelsey said.

"Speak for yourself," Jessica said. "I expect pampering from now on."

"Ryan's part is almost done," Tyler said.

"So I can take care of you and the babies," Ryan said happily.

"Twins," Jessica said, shaking her head.

"You keep saying that," Ryan commented.

"I'll be saying it for the next thirty weeks," Jessica replied.

"You'll get used to it," Ryan said, kissing her on the lips.

"Never," Jessica said, as a staff member walked over.

"Sir, dinner is served," the steward said to Tyler.

The couples sat at a round table with a low centerpiece of roses and orchids, and within two minutes they were served beautiful green salads, which were accented with edible flowers. Tyler fed Kelsey from his fork while he looked into her eyes. Kelsey smiled. She had missed this Tyler, happy and carefree, and she was thrilled to have him back.

"Thank you," Kelsey said, after she chewed.

"Thank you," Tyler replied. He ran his free hand through her loose hair.

"Can I really eat this?" Jessica asked Ryan from across the table. She had picked one of the flowers off the food.

"It's fine," Ryan replied. "Not the nasturtium, though." He picked the large orange nasturtium off her plate, and placed it on Kelsey's.

"Why not?" Tyler asked.

"It's not good for pregnant women," Ryan said firmly.

"I can't eat anything," Jessica said.

"Of course you can. You just have to be careful. And eat nutritious food," Ryan replied, picking up a crostini.

"Fine, I can't eat anything good," Jessica replied, taking a bite of her salad.

"It's only for a few months. Anyway, you want our babies to be healthy."

"I do," Jessica said. She rubbed her tummy gently, and Ryan beamed at her.

"You've made Ryan very, very happy," Tyler commented, offering Kelsey a ciabatta-topped crostini. She took a bite.

"Very," Ryan said, gently stroking Jessica's face.

"I'm happy too. Just a little nervous," Jessica said.

"I don't blame you. They might turn out like Ryan," Tyler commented. Ryan glared at him, and Jessica laughed.

"You'll be a great mom," Kelsey said.

"Notice she didn't say you'll be a good father," Tyler said to Ryan.

"I'm going to be a great father," Ryan retorted. "You'll wish you were as awesome as I'm going to be."

Tyler laughed. "We'll see," he said. "It doesn't matter, you'll have a dozen nannies anyway."

Ryan shook his head. "I don't want a nanny for the babies."

Jessica gave him a look of surprise. "Are you kidding me?"

"No," Ryan said.

"Yes, you are," Jessica said. "We're calling in reinforcements. There's no way we can take care of twins by ourselves."

"We'll see."

"No, we won't," Jessica said. "We're getting a nanny. And you can stop pouting."

"Maybe," Ryan said, taking a bite of his salad.

"Just give in. Anyway, you've got to go to work," Tyler said.

"Not after the kids are born," Ryan said.

"What?" Tyler said.

"Bob said we could stay home if we wanted to."

"Stay at home with two kids? Count me out," Jessica said.

"I might want to," Ryan replied.

"Fine, you can be a house-husband. I'd go crazy," Jessica said, taking a crostini covered with tapenade.

"You're leaving your kids in Ryan's hands?" Tyler teased.

"Quiet, you," Ryan replied.

Tyler shrugged and fed Kelsey another bite of salad.

After the salad, they were served a delicious minestrone soup, then the entree, pesto pasta with salmon.

"Did Ryan tell you what to order?" Jessica asked, as she stirred her pasta. "Suddenly, I'm eating a lot of salmon."

"It's good for the babies," Ryan said.

"Maybe I'll move to Bob's for a few months and eat what I want to," Jessica commented.

"No, you won't."

"Ryan, you don't want me to eat sugar, peanuts, coffee, tea, red meat, or raw fish."

"None of that is good for the babies," Ryan said.

"Some of it might be good for me," Jessica replied.

"It's only a few months," Ryan said.

"You can eat what you want," Jessica said.

"I'll eat what you eat. Support you," Ryan replied. Jessica frowned and Kelsey and Tyler smiled at each other. That wasn't the answer that Jessica wanted to hear. Jessica stabbed a piece of salmon and ate it.

"Ryan, you should let Jess eat a few of those things," Kelsey said. "Not all of those things are bad for pregnant women in moderation."

"See. Kelsey's a biology major. She knows," Jessica said.

"OK," Ryan said. "What on my list can she eat?"

"I don't think anyone recommends that pregnant women totally avoid sugar or red meat," Kelsey said.

"I was hoping you would say I could have coffee," Jessica said.

"Not in the first trimester," Kelsey replied.

Jessica sighed. "At least I don't drink. That's one less thing I have to give up," she said.

"You'll be happy later," Ryan said brightly.

Tyler spent most of the meal looking at Kelsey, stroking her face and hair, and sneaking kisses. Kelsey felt so loved, and was grateful to be with her friends and her Tyler.

Kelsey was amused when they were served a fruit-sweetened raspberry sorbet at the end of the meal.

Jessica frowned. "Seriously?"

"You can have sugar twice a week if Kelsey says it's OK," Ryan said unconcernedly.

"I can have sugar for every meal if I say so," Jessica retorted.

"Jess, it's not good for them," Ryan replied.

"Moderation," Kelsey said to Jessica.

"Papa Jefferson says so," Tyler whispered to Kelsey and she laughed.

Tyler held Kelsey in his arms as the yacht glided through Puget Sound. Ryan and Jess were on the other side of the boat, having a private moment of their own.

"You realize that our engagement is the worst-kept secret in the world, right?" Kelsey said to him.

"It isn't a secret," Tyler said decisively.

"It's not?"

"No. It's just easier for everyone if I am the one to tell Lisa, and I'd prefer not to do that before I send her the proxy letter. But if she finds out, I'll just move up the date of the letter, and deal with her then."

"Then I hope you're prepared to do that," Kelsey mused. "Right now, all staff here and at the Fairmont know about it, as well as everyone in the office."

"And all of them have a duty of confidentiality," Tyler replied. "It's fine, anyway, it wouldn't be the first time that my engagement was announced prematurely."

Kelsey looked at Tyler in shock, and he laughed at the look on her face.

"I wasn't engaged," Tyler commented. "But one of the tabloids claimed that I was."

"Oh," Kelsey said, with more relief than she expected.

"I'm not marrying anyone but you," Tyler said.

"I'm starting to see that," Kelsey replied.

"You mean everything to me," Tyler said.

"I know. You mean everything to me too," Kelsey replied. She adjusted herself in Tyler's arms and he held her a little tighter.

On Sunday, Tyler picked Kelsey up in his car, and after several deep and romantic kisses, they drove onto I-5.

"So where are we going?" Kelsey asked curiously.

"It's a surprise," Tyler replied.

"It's always a surprise," Kelsey said testily.

Tyler laughed. "I thought you liked my surprises," he commented.

"Your surprises are getting more complicated. It worries me," Kelsey said honestly.

"This isn't a complicated one," Tyler said. "We're going to Tacoma."

"Tacoma?" Kelsey asked curiously. "What's in Tacoma?" Tyler and Zach had studied for the bar exam there, and Zach had said that Kelsey should visit the glass museum, but Kelsey had never been, and wasn't sure what else there was to see.

"There's a lot in Tacoma," Tyler replied. "The owner of the breakfast restaurant that Zach used to drag me to commented that people in Tacoma think nothing of driving up to Seattle, but Seattleites think that the hour to drive to Tacoma is an hour too much."

"So what are we doing?" Kelsey asked, settling back in her seat.

"Patience, Miss North," Tyler teased.

"You know I have none, Mr. Olsen," Kelsey replied.

"I don't know about that," Tyler said.

"Well, waiting for you was different," Kelsey said.

"Why?" Tyler asked curiously.

Kelsey thought for a moment. "Because you're special to me."

"Am I?"

"Very much."

"You're special to me too."

"I know," Kelsey said.

"I'm glad you do. You didn't forget while we were apart, did you?"

"Nope," Kelsey replied.

"Good. Because I love you."

"I love you too," Kelsey said, glancing at him as they passed King County International Airport. Kelsey wondered if Bob's plane was parked there today.

"I'm really sorry, Kelsey."

"About what?"

"About my life," Tyler said.

"What about your life?" Kelsey asked curiously.

"If my life was normal, you wouldn't have had to go through this," Tyler explained. "I could have been like everyone else, with an ordinary family, and we could have just fallen in love and gotten married, and told anyone who got in our way to pound sand."

"Tyler, if your life was normal, you wouldn't be you," Kelsey replied. "I'm in love with you. Not some ordinary guy."

Tyler smiled, but kept his eyes on the road. "You make me so happy, you know that too, right?" he finally said.

"I know," Kelsey replied blissfully.

"Tell me about our wedding," Tyler said.

"What do you mean?"

"Jess knew exactly what she wanted for her wedding to Ryan. So I'm wondering what you want for ours."

"You saw what I showed to Morgan," Kelsey said. Tyler had been in the room when she and Morgan had shown each other their wedding ideas.

"I did. Is that all?"

"I guess so. I haven't really thought about it," Kelsey said.

"You should. We're getting married soon."

"This summer."

"Or sooner."

"No," Kelsey replied.

Tyler sighed. "Anyway," he said, "You should think about it."

"Maybe later," Kelsey replied. "I have other things to think about."

"Like our wedding night?" Tyler asked.

Kelsey blushed scarlet. "No, I'm definitely not thinking about that," she managed to say.

"Interesting, I can think about little else," Tyler said coolly.

"Try," Kelsey ordered.

"Unlikely," Tyler replied

"Tyler. You're making me uncomfortable," Kelsey admitted.

"Sorry," Tyler said, as they changed lanes.

"It's OK. Let's just change the subject for now."

"So what is on the approved list of conversation topics?" Tyler asked.

"We could talk about work."

"We're always there. I don't want to talk about work," Tyler replied.

"How about Becks?"

"She's a pain, but a necessary one. That's really all I have to say about her."

"Ryan and Jess?"

"Ryan is still annoying, although Jess is glowing these days."

"It's the pregnancy hormones. Plus she's thrilled about the babies."

"I am happy for them."

"Me, too. Jess wants to go baby shopping next weekend."

"Already?" Tyler asked.

"These are going to be the most pampered babies on the planet," Kelsey said.

"True. Ryan asked me to be a godfather for them."

"Really? Did you say yes?"

"Of course. I guess I should get my checkbook out."

"Why?"

"Isn't the godparent's job to buy gifts?"

"I thought it was teach the child about religion? Give them a moral compass?"

"Ryan's kids?"

"I would think that they would need that guidance more than most," Kelsey said deadpan.

Tyler laughed. "You're right. I'd better start preparing. Lesson one, developing common sense."

Kelsey giggled. "So I have a question for you. Why does Ryan 'owe you'?"

"Owe me what?" Tyler asked.

"When you told us about Ryan's condo, Ryan said that he owed you. Why does he think that?"

"Because for about ten years of my life, my job was to get Ryan out of the various problems he had managed to get into."

"Like what?"

"Like everything."

"I thought that was Ryan's lawyer's job?" Kelsey said.

"I'm the first line of defense. My job is to solve the problem before he has to call his lawyer," Tyler replied.

"I see. So how many times have you helped him?"

Tyler looked thoughtful as he drove. "About sixty."

"Sixty?"

"Once every couple of months, over ten years," Tyler said. "Maybe more like ninety."

Kelsey burst out into laughter. "You're kidding!"

"Ryan is a problem," Tyler replied.

"He isn't any more," Kelsey said.

"That what you think. Just because he's staying on this side of the law, doesn't mean he's not a thorn in my side," Tyler replied.

"Is that why you weren't talking to him?" Kelsey asked seriously.

"I wasn't talking to Ryan because I couldn't bear to see him happy when I wasn't," Tyler replied. Kelsey understood. She liked spending time with Ryan and Jess after she and Tyler broke up because it gave her hope, but she could see why Tyler would feel the opposite.

"Will you be OK going back to Tacoma?" Kelsey asked. She suspected, without knowing for sure, that some of Tyler's darkest days had been spent there.

"That's why we're going. I need to have some better memories of the city," Tyler replied.

"I think we can make that happen," Kelsey said optimistically.

"I'm sure we can," Tyler replied.

"How's Zach?" Kelsey asked.

"Stressed out. Between work, trying to juggle three girlfriends, and sneaking around to find out confidential Tactec information around his parents' office, he's pretty busy."

"What is he trying to find out?" Kelsey asked.

"I'm trying to figure out how badly Tactec has mishandled the Koh Software merger, and Zach and Ryan are trying to get some information for me."

"Isn't it all in the paper?" Kelsey asked. Tactec's bungling of the merger was national news, and Kelsey knew from Jess that Lisa Olsen was back from California.

"I think the problems are deeper than Lisa is admitting."

"You can't disclose any confidential Tactec information during the proxy fight, though," Kelsey said.

"I know, but I want to know what's actually happening. It will give me leverage with Lisa later."

"Leverage?" Kelsey asked.

"When she's fighting with me about the board," Tyler clarified.

"Of course," Kelsey said. Occasionally, she forgot that Tyler's proxy battle wasn't just about her. It was also about the shareholders of Tactec.

"Lisa's not going to give up those board seats without a fight, but I want her to start thinking about why Koh Software wouldn't have turned out so badly if she had smarter board members."

"Why wouldn't it have?" Kelsey asked.

"Because Lisa wouldn't have bought Koh." Tyler replied.

Kelsey thought for a moment. This summer, Bob had mentioned that Tyler had been against the merger, but she hadn't talked about it with

Tyler. Now seemed like the perfect time.

"Why were you against the merger?" Kelsey asked. "Bob said that you were."

"Because Rick Burton is a jerk," Tyler said. "He loves control and hates women. He was never going to let Lisa run his company."

"How did you know that?" Kelsey asked.

"Fewer than 15% of the employees at Koh Software are women, and he has exactly one woman engineer. All of the other women are in HR or Marketing, or somewhere in the company where they have no voice in product development."

"Really?" Kelsey said.

"I thought it was a sign of an underlying problem. Lisa didn't. And by the time it mattered, Lisa had stopped listening to me."

"She's paying for it now," Kelsey commented.

"That she is. She hates California," Tyler replied. "And because she's dealing with Rick Burton, she's there every few weeks."

"Why hasn't she been able to get him under control? Why doesn't she just fire him?" Kelsey asked.

"Because Lisa has deluded herself into believing that she can use her charm or her money to get her out of any situation. It's not going to work this time."

"What will?" Kelsey asked.

"I'm not sure. I haven't met him, so I don't know what motivates him," Tyler said. "But I'm pretty sure that Lisa's not going to be the catalyst to make things right. She's the problem, not the solution. But her ego's not going to admit that."

Kelsey rarely spoke to Tyler about his mother's business dealings, but she was always fascinated when she did. Despite everything, Kelsey still admired Lisa Olsen, and the fact that she and Bob had created a multi-billion-dollar business from nothing.

"What about Bob? Do you think that it would help if Bob went to talk to him? Man to man?"

"Bob's been to California, but Rick knows where the power lies, and he knows it's not with Bob."

"What would you do?"

"It's not my problem."

"Yes, but I bet you have a solution," Kelsey replied.

"Lisa needs to get out of the business of integrating startups into Tactec," Tyler said. "She doesn't have time to deal with them when things go wrong, and things usually do."

"Who would do it then?" Kelsey asked.

"She should designate someone to do it. Maybe someone who reports to the head of legal," Tyler replied. "Then Lisa could watch over what was happening, but not be as visibly responsible when everything goes south."

"What does the board have to do with the failure of Koh's integration into Tactec?"

"They should have told Lisa no," Tyler said bluntly. "But they didn't, because they never do."

"And your board members would have?" Kelsey knew the general biographies of Tyler's proposed board members, but she hadn't met them, and Tyler hadn't discussed them much.

"I believe so. I think the problems would have been obvious if anyone had been paying attention, and at the very least, the board members I'm proposing have industry experience."

"Have any of them met Rick Burton?"

"Two, but neither of them know him well," Tyler replied. "However, the third, Victoria Grant, said that when she read about the merger she had a bad feeling, because Rick has a reputation around Silicon Valley for being difficult to work with. She couldn't imagine that he would be able to put that aside to work with Lisa."

"Too bad that she wasn't on the board at the time," Kelsey said.

"And she probably won't be next time either," Tyler admitted. "But it's worth a shot."

"Can I ask another question?"

"Yes, but you don't have to ask," Tyler said.

"I only ask when the next question is particularly nosy," Kelsey said.

"I see," Tyler said with a grin. "Go ahead."

"Why are you borrowing the money from Ryan?"

"From a tax standpoint, it was the easiest way," Tyler replied.

Kelsey looked at Tyler doubtfully.

"And I knew Lisa wouldn't like it," Tyler admitted.

"That sounds like you," Kelsey said.

"Actually though, I would have needed to borrow the money from somewhere, and I didn't really want to explain what I was doing to my trustees. The only collateral I have is tied up in one trust or another. Ryan just got a bank loan against the condo, no questions asked."

"That makes sense then. Is this really going to cost four million dollars?"

"I hope not. But probably," Tyler replied.

"How will you pay Ryan back? Out of your trusts?"

"I didn't want to discuss this before we got married, but as you know, Washington is a community property state, which means that I'm entitled to half of your salary when we get married," Tyler teased.

Kelsey laughed. "Funny. I don't think that half of my salary is going to pay off a four-million-dollar loan."

"Don't you own an office building?" Tyler asked.

"I'm holding it for you. Can I give it back to you?" Kelsey asked seriously.

"It's yours," Tyler replied.

"You could use it for the proxy fight."

"No, I can't," Tyler replied. "If it turns out I need to pay Ryan back, I'll make arrangements."

"What do you mean if you need to pay Ryan back?"

"If by some miracle, I win the proxy fight, I'll request that Tactec reimburse me."

"Can they do that?"

"Sure," Tyler said. "Particularly if I have my three candidates on the board."

"What do you think your chances of winning are?"

"Five, ten percent," Tyler said. "My winning means one of three things. Either Lisa or Bob votes for me, and I think that the chances of that are exactly zero, or I'm so convincing to the shareholders that every single one of them votes for my candidates. Considering Becks' comments this week, I think that's pretty unlikely too. Maybe my chances of winning are one percent or less."

"I still support you," Kelsey said.

"I depend on that," Tyler replied.

They were quiet for a while, as they zipped down I-5 towards Tacoma. The expressway wasn't crowded at this time of day, and Kelsey was enjoying seeing parts of the state that she hadn't seen before.

"So what do you think the twins will be? Boys or girls?" Tyler asked.

"Or both," Kelsey reminded him.

"True. That would be interesting," Tyler said. "Jess should be hoping for girls."

Kelsey giggled. "Jess figures that with five kids, one of them is going to turn out like Ryan. I think she's serious about bringing in the Marines."

"Jeffrey told me that Bob is in a panic about losing his youth. He bought a MacLaren."

"What's a MacLaren?"

"A very expensive sports car that Ryan is hoping to get his hands on," Tyler explained.

"Did I tell you that Bob bought Morgan a car for Christmas?"

"No, really?"

"A red Corvette."

"Nice. Morgan must be pleased."

Kelsey bit her lip, but she decided to tell Tyler about Fiona. She wasn't exactly a secret.

"When I was in Arizona, I met Bob's girlfriend there," Kelsey said. Tyler glanced at Kelsey, with a bit of surprise. "Morgan thinks that the car is an apology."

"You met Fiona?" Tyler said.

"Yes, have you?"

"No. I didn't even know her name until Jeffrey slipped up last summer," Tyler replied. "Is Morgan OK?"

"Morgan knew about her, so she's fine."

"But?" Tyler said wisely.

"I think Morgan is trying to figure out why Bob won't choose between them," Kelsey said. Morgan hadn't articulated this conclusion, but in talking to her, Kelsey thought it was true. "Why is Bob continuing to date Morgan, when it's pretty clear that he's not going to marry her?"

"I will never understand Bob," Tyler said. "I think that the fact that Ryan disapproves so strongly of Morgan is the reason he hasn't asked her, though."

"Is it really Morgan's age?" Kelsey asked.

"Ryan thinks that if he complains enough, Bob won't get remarried. He's wrong. Ryan should stop whining and let Bob marry Morgan."

"Why is he still going out with Fiona?"

"I don't know. Maybe it's his way of not leading Morgan on. If he has two girlfriends, she'll expect less from him. And that would give Bob the space to deal with Ryan."

"Do you think Ryan's going to change his mind?"

"No," Tyler said. "Ryan wants Bob to settle into the role of doting grandfather to his kids. He doesn't want Bob to start building a new relationship with wife number five. Ryan's a selfish jerk."

"Do you think so? How would you react if Lisa got remarried?" Kelsey asked.

"LIsa's not getting remarried," Tyler replied.

"Why are you so sure?" Kelsey asked.

"I don't think Lisa's the marrying kind. Look at the guys she's been dating," Tyler said. Kelsey knew that Lisa had turned down a proposal, so perhaps Tyler was right.

"Anyway, it's Lisa's life. It has nothing to do with me," Tyler concluded.

"I suppose that's true."

"That's why I don't get Ryan. He never has to see Bob's wife if he doesn't want to. He's managed to avoid his own mother for years. Why shouldn't Bob be happy? Ryan is."

"I don't know. I think I wouldn't be happy if one of my parents was planning on getting remarried."

"Kels, Bob's been married four times. Ryan's used to it. He's just causing trouble because he doesn't have anything else to do," Tyler concluded.

After another interlude of quiet, Tyler suggested that they come up with baby names for the twins, and Kelsey was happy to play along. By the time they had jokingly settled on names like Tyler Davis Olsen Perkins the eighth, and Hydronic Perkins Jr., Tyler had pulled off I-5 and into the city of Tacoma.

Kelsey looked around in interest. Tacoma was an industrial city, and there were historical buildings all along the route into town. After a couple of minutes, Tyler pulled into a parking spot on the street. As he did so, Kelsey caught a glimpse of a sign for the University of Washington Tacoma Campus.

"This is it," Tyler said, removing his keys. He and Kelsey got out of the car, just as the light rail cars rumbled past them. Kelsey looked up at the building they were parked in front of, as Tyler walked around the car, and took Kelsey's hand, and gave her a kiss. Her ring sparkled in the winter sun.

"The Washington State History Museum?" Kelsey said.

"This is the Museum District. The History Museum, The Museum of Glass, and The Tacoma Art Museum are all here. I thought we'd go to all three."

"Awesome," Kelsey said. She had wanted to go to the Museum of Glass ever since Zach had mentioned how beautiful it was last summer.

Tyler nuzzled her neck. "Or we could get back in the car and make out."

Kelsey looked at him, and he looked back with innocent eyes.

"You're waiting until this summer. Unless there are any more delays."

"No more delays, Princess. We're getting married," Tyler said, and he kissed her hand.

A half-hour later, Tyler held Kelsey around the waist as she looked in delight at a gigantic model railroad.

"This is so cool," Kelsey said happily.

"I didn't know that you liked trains," Tyler replied.

"I do. I didn't see them often as a kid," Kelsey replied.

"I guess there isn't a train in Port Townsend," Tyler said.

"Nope," Kelsey replied, as she looked at the railroad scene. "Look at the 50's style car," she said excitedly, pointing as one of the trains rolled by.

"You're like a little kid," Tyler said, kissing her hair.

"I'm just happy to be with you," Kelsey replied.

"Me too," Tyler said, nuzzling her again.

After a visit to the Great Hall of Washington History, where Kelsey and Tyler spent two hours walking through interactive exhibits which showcased the stories of the growth and the people of Washington, they walked outside and out into the plaza.

"Which museum next?" Kelsey asked, swinging hands with Tyler.

"The Museum of Glass," Tyler replied. He looked at her with his sparkling brown eyes.

"It's really nice here," Kelsey said, looking at the wide street as they headed away from the History Museum.

"I like Tacoma a lot," Tyler agreed.

"People in Seattle don't seem to think much of it," Kelsey said.

"They're missing out," Tyler said. "Next time, we should take the Sounder train. I didn't realize that you were such a train fan."

"I've only ridden light rail in Portland and Seattle. I haven't been on a train trip," Kelsey said.

"Maybe we should do that for our honeymoon. A long train trip. A bedroom for two in the sleeper car," Tyler said dreamily.

"Maybe not," Kelsey said, snapping him out of his reverie.

"Where do you want to go?" Tyler asked. "Paris?"

Kelsey shook her head.

"Tell me," Tyler said.

"Later," Kelsey said.

"Now. It will give me something to think about, because the only thing I can picture is you and me in a locked bedroom for days."

Kelsey giggled. "Italy," she said.

"Really?" Tyler said.

"I think that would be great," Kelsey said. Her heart skipped as she said it. Could she dare to dream that she and Tyler would be married, and go on a honeymoon together? After all they had been through, after all of the time they had been apart, one day would they really be together as husband and wife?

"I'm not sure I would have expected that," Tyler said.

"Why?"

"I didn't know you were interested in Italy."

"Two words. Italian food," Kelsey replied.

Tyler laughed. "Oh, I see. Now it all makes sense."

"Plus, there's so much art, I thought you would like it too."

"The only statuesque body I'll be interested in on the honeymoon is yours," Tyler replied and Kelsey blushed scarlet.

The couple walked hand-in-hand through the Chihuly Bridge of Glass, with was filled with colorful glass art. Kelsey stretched her head back as she looked at all of the beautiful pieces which were displayed on the ceiling. She marveled at the fact that she had seen similar pieces in Tyler's childhood home.

They took their time as they strolled through the museum. Neither of them knew much about glass art, as Tyler's father worked in wood, and Kelsey had only started regularly going to art museums after she met Tyler. So both of them were fascinated by what the museum had to offer. They sat for almost an hour watching glass artists blow vases in the museum's 'hot shop', a space dedicated to the creation of new works of glass art. Then they walked through the numerous exhibits.

As darkness began to fall, they walked back through the Chihuly Bridge of Glass, which was now illuminated. When they stepped back onto the sidewalk and back into downtown, the cool winter air blew through Kelsey's hair. But she felt as warm as the sun.

After another hour at the Tacoma Art Museum, their third museum for the day, they crossed Pacific Avenue and began walking back up the street.

"Zach and I lived here," Tyler said, pointing up at a historic building which looked as if it had been converted into apartments.

Kelsey looked up, blinking from the bright street light, then she looked at Tyler, who had a faraway look on his face.

"That, was without question, one of the worst times of my life," Tyler said in a serious tone. "And not just because I was living with Zach," he quipped.

Kelsey couldn't help but giggle. "Tyler," she protested. "I thought you were serious."

"I was. I missed you so much, and I didn't know when I'd see you again," Tyler said. "But here we are, and everything makes sense again."

"It does," Kelsey agreed.

"If you don't have a preference, I'll like to take you here," Tyler said as they stopped in front of a fusion Asian restaurant.

Kelsey looked inside the glass windows. "Sure," she said. "Is this one of the places you ate when you lived here?"

"No," Tyler said. Kelsey glanced at him, then she realized. Tyler had been struggling with his eating disorder when he was here with Zach.

"I did eat," he clarified, "Just not here. I wanted to save it for you."

Kelsey felt tears come to her eyes, and impulsively she hugged Tyler tightly. Tyler held her and they stood outside, grateful to be together.

They shared a delicious meal together, full of fresh Asian vegetables and amazing flavor combinations. Tyler fed Kelsey coconut prawns, and Kelsey fed Tyler beef noodles, and they delighted in each other's company.

After dinner, they walked across the street. But instead of heading to the car, Tyler led Kelsey to a small park next to the Washington State History Museum and they sat on one of the wooden benches in the cool evening air. Kelsey leaned her head against Tyler's shoulder, and they sat there for a moment, before Tyler finally spoke.

"I need to know what she knows," Tyler said.

He didn't have to explain. Kelsey knew exactly what Tyler was asking.

Kelsey sat up and looked into Tyler's eyes in the darkness. She had known this day would come.

As she looked at Tyler, she wondered why she had put it off for so long. She believed that Tyler wouldn't judge her any more than she had judged herself.

She began without preamble.

"When I was twelve, my family was having a hard time. The store wasn't doing well, and my parents were fighting a lot. It was a difficult time for me. I wasn't sure what to do.

"So I started drinking.

"At the time, Jasmine was excited about starting high school and Morgan was busy dealing with the chaos of her own life, so I started hanging out with Eric. I had had a crush on Eric forever, because he was older, and to my teenage mind, very cool, but Eric saw me as a little sister. He was happy to let me hang out though, so I took advantage.

"Eric pretty much had his own place. His mother had left ages ago, and Eric's father was almost never home, so his house became a escape. I

241

could go there any time, drink from Eric's father's stash and forget about what was happening at home. And I did.

"At first, it was a once-a-week thing, then every few days, then every afternoon. My grades fell and I spent less time with Jasmine and Morgan. My parents knew something was wrong, but they had no idea what to do. All of their friends' daughters were still playing with their Barbies. It went on for months, off and on.

"I knew what I was doing, I knew I wasn't supposed to being doing it, and I did it anyway.

"I went to high school, and joined the track team. That lasted about nine weeks, until I got dropped. I had gone to practice drunk.

"When I got kicked off the team, that was pretty much the end of the little stability I had. One night I decided to sneak out of the house and go see Eric. I took my mom's car, but I had already been drinking. I wrapped my mom's car around a tree three blocks from our house. When I woke up in the hospital, I had a broken leg, and one of the highest blood alcohol levels the doctors had seen in someone my age.

"So now, the law was involved. And that was the beginning of the new me.

"The prosecutor threw the book at me. I was charged with joyriding — a felony in Washington — driving without a license, driving while intoxicated, vandalism, and everything else they could think of. My family couldn't afford a lawyer at the time, so I was assigned a public defender. I was terrified, because I thought they were going to make an example out of me.

"Until the accident, no one really knew how bad things were. I had never been the best student, and the teen years are difficult for a lot of people, but this was clearly different. The community rallied around my parents and me. Several of my teachers and neighbors wrote letters to the court, and the prosecutor and public defender agreed to a plea deal.

242

"I spent a weekend in the juvenile jail, had to work in my family's store to pay them back for the car, and I had to do community service to make amends for the neighbor's tree. I also was told that I had to attend AA meetings weekly for the next three years.

"Jasmine's family took me in for three months, so my parents could work on their own lives. Jazz, Morgan, and my friend Matt all swore not to drink alcohol until we became 21. Actually, I don't think Jasmine still has ever had a drink. Morgan's aunt gave me free therapy sessions. The neighbor whose tree I destroyed became my AA sponsor. She told me that it was my life, and I could choose to live it in either the right way or the wrong way, but it was always my choice.

"And slowly, things got better."

"What happened to Eric?" Tyler asked her. Of course, Tyler had met him the last Christmas they had gone home.

"My father and Morgan's dad paid him a visit and told him that he'd better start carding his guests from now on. Eric told me that Morgan's dad brought his hunting rifle along. As did mine."

Kelsey sighed. "So now you know the old Kelsey."

Tyler smiled at her. "You never do things halfway, do you?" he asked.

Kelsey laughed, and she felt her nervousness fall away. "Never," she replied.

"No wonder Lisa reacted the way she did. She's never even gotten a traffic ticket."

"I should have told you. But my record was expunged. No one is supposed to see it."

"They don't throw it in the trash, Kels."

"I guess I was hoping they did," Kelsey replied.

"Ryan has an expunged record too. I think his was actually thrown in the trash though. Or burned."

"What did Ryan do?" Kelsey asked.

"What hasn't Ryan done?" Tyler answered. "Did you expunge it yourself?"

"A lawyer in Port Townsend helped me when I was 18. Now I'm a little nervous, though."

"My mother doesn't go through normal channels. I'm sure it's hidden from everyone else unless they're looking for it specifically."

"That's good," Kelsey paused, and looked at Tyler in the dark. "What do you think?" Kelsey asked him.

"About what?" Tyler replied.

"About me. About what I did."

"Are you kidding? That used to be a fun weekend for Ryan," Tyler said.

"I'm not Ryan," Kelsey said.

"No, you're my Princess. So all I care about is that you're all right. Which you clearly are. It was a long time ago. "

"It doesn't matter to you?"

"Do you think it should?" Tyler asked.

Kelsey pondered this. "Maybe," she admitted.

"I'm sorry, it doesn't. Although I didn't know the details, you've been open about your imperfections. Much more than I have."

"You're perfect," Kelsey interjected.

"Hardly."

"To me you are," Kelsey replied.

"That's the way I feel about you. Your past is what has made you my Kelsey. I can accept that, as long as I get to be in your future. So that's what I need to work on."

"How?"

"I need to talk to Lisa," Tyler said. "She can be reasoned with."

"She hasn't been too willing to talk to you lately," Kelsey pointed out.

"Remember, I'm about to give her an incentive to do so," Tyler replied.

Kelsey leaned her head back against Tyler and he caressed her. She felt his gentle breathing through his fleece jacket.

"You really don't care about what I did," Kelsey said, mostly to herself.

"No," Tyler said, kissing her.

That night, after Tyler had driven her home, Kelsey lay in bed and looked up at her ceiling. She felt that a weight had been lifted from her, a weight she hadn't realized had been there.

For all of this time, ever since she had fallen in love with Tyler Olsen, she had wondered what he would think, what he would say when she revealed her secret. In her heart, she had hoped that he would take it well, but for years there had always been a touch of doubt.

Would he stop loving her? Would he decide that her past would end their future?

But tonight, Tyler had proven to Kelsey that he was the one she always thought he was. Someone who could look at her past and accept that it didn't define her.

Someone who could love Kelsey not despite, but because of, her flaws. The flaws that made her the person she was today.

Kelsey looked up at the ceiling, and a lone tear slid into her pillow.

Today, Kelsey realized, she understood true love.

Promptly at 8 p.m. on Monday, Rebecca Jones walked into the small conference room where Kelsey and Tyler were waiting. The couple had finished dinner, and Tyler had just returned from removing their trash.

As she had been previously, Ms. Jones was immaculate in her suit. This time, her suit was a bold red, and she sat at the table confidently after Tyler stood and shook her hand.

"Changed your mind?" Ms. Jones asked, surveying Tyler.

"No," Tyler said.

"Unfortunate," Ms. Jones replied. "All right, we'll get started. Have you ever done a formal interview with the media before?"

"No, I haven't."

"I'm surprised. You're Lisa Olsen's son."

"I'm not interested in media attention. I mean, until now."

"You think you have a private life?"

"I try to," Tyler replied.

"You won't any more," Rebecca Jones said bluntly. "Are you OK with that?"

Tyler looked thoughtful for a moment. "I'll have to be. This has to be done," he finally replied.

"As long as you understand that this will probably change everything for you. You've flown under the radar for a long time, but you're inviting the media into your life. You're attempting to set the boundaries, and force the media to focus on your proxy fight, but there's a good chance that they are going to ignore you, and tell the story that they want to tell. I'm going to do what you can, so your story is in the spotlight, but the minute you speak to your first reporter, you are handing over control."

Tyler nodded. "I understand," he replied.

Kelsey watched their exchange with interest. For as long as she had known Tyler, he had guarded his privacy zealously. Although Tyler had been friendly with everyone in law school, he had only been friends with a select few. Kelsey knew for a fact that Tyler had no issue with suing reporters and bloggers, in order to keep his private life private. But now he was practically daring the media to dig into his life. Like Ms. Jones had said, once Tyler opened the door, everything was fair game.

Everything — including Kelsey.

"So tonight, we're just going to talk. Every Monday, between now and your first real interview, you and I will sit here for an hour, and practice. But tonight we need to plan your strategy, and decide what you need to work on most."

"Ms. Jones?" Kelsey said. Ms. Jones looked at Kelsey. "Do I need to do anything but observe?"

"No," Ms. Jones replied. "I do want you to pay attention. You'll be traveling with Tyler, and you will need to able to coach him on his presentation when I'm otherwise occupied, or when he's practicing here or at home. And I do expect you to practice, Mr. Olsen," Ms. Jones said pointedly. "By the way, the two of you can call me Becks. Bill's never going to stop, so you might as well use the same nickname."

"How do you know Bill?" Tyler asked.

"We went to high school together," Becks replied. Kelsey and Tyler looked at each other. It was hard to imagine Bill Simon as a high school student. "Everyone called me Becks then. OK, Tyler. What do you know about preparing for media interviews?"

"Only what I've read," Tyler replied.

"You haven't seen your mother prepare for them?"

"I have, but I wasn't really paying attention," Tyler replied honestly.

"You lived with the master of media manipulation, and you didn't learn anything?" Becks said.

"No," Tyler said with a laugh.

"Lisa Olsen is very good at getting the media to write the story that she wants to read," Becks commented. "We'd better hope that she doesn't want to write the story of her awful son."

"I'm confident that she won't," Tyler said. Kelsey was less sure. She knew that Tyler meant a lot to his mother, but Kelsey wasn't sure that would be enough to stop an angry Lisa Olsen.

"You have 27 words, nine seconds, and three key ideas," Becks said, beginning the lesson. "So your only job during every interview is to make sure that you get those three key ideas in front of the audience. I've taken the liberty of preparing your three key ideas, so let's start with that. First, you are initiating this proxy fight on your mother's behalf, because you believe that she deserves a better board." Becks looked at Tyler firmly. "You believe that, don't you?" she challenged.

"I do," Tyler replied. Kelsey couldn't read Tyler's look. She knew that the main reason for the proxy fight had little to do with the board, and a lot to do with Tyler's relationship with Lisa, but Kelsey also realized that even when Tyler and Lisa were getting along, the Tactec board was a thorn in Tyler's side. So perhaps Tyler honestly did believe that a better board was good for Lisa.

"Second, you believe that an improved board is better for the long-term health of the company." Becks paused to see if there was disagreement from Tyler. Seeing none, she went on. "Third, you believe that an improved board is better for shareholder value. That's it."

"That's all?" Kelsey asked.

"That's all. Of course Tyler will back up each of those points with data and detailed explanations if anyone is listening, but no one will be. Instead, every reporter who talks to Tyler will be trying to figure out whether Tyler is serious about the proxy fight, coming up with comparisons to his mother, or laughing at his nerve to go against Tactec. The best we can hope for is that these very simple messages come across, and that's going to be Tyler's job. So Mr. Olsen, are those key points acceptable to you?"

"Yes, those are fine," Tyler said. Kelsey could tell from his look that Tyler wanted to say more when he was speaking to the media, but with only 27 words, it was clear to all of them that the message needed to be to the point.

"Tyler, you know I think this is a really bad idea," Becks said, surveying him.

"I know," Tyler said unconcernedly.

"But you don't care."

"I respect your opinion, but I know Lisa Olsen very well. She's not going to listen unless someone forces her to. By creating a debate in the media, she's going to be forced to consider some changes, even if they aren't the exact ones I want to make," Tyler replied.

"That's fair," Becks conceded. "I'm going to keep challenging you on this, up until the moment you send the letter over to Tactec. You need to understand what you're getting into, and I'm not sure that you do."

"I'm not sure that I do either," Tyler agreed. "But here we go."

Becks returned on Thursday evening, and the day's lesson was on how to speak. Kelsey thought that Tyler would have no trouble with this, but Tyler had pointed out that it was one thing to give a speech to hundreds of people, and something else entirely to have a one-on-one discussion with someone who was going to be skeptical of your motives and had a vested interest in tripping you up.

"Smile, Tyler," Becks said. She wasn't smiling at all. "Your mother is known for her charm, so you need to be at least as pleasant as she is, otherwise the story will be about the grumpy heir."

Tyler smiled.

"Better," Becks said. "So Mr. Olsen, why are you beginning this proxy fight now?"

"After the problems with the Koh Software integration, I'm concerned…"

"Slower," Becks ordered.

Tyler sighed, and began again.

"After the problems with the Koh Software integration…"

"Don't forget to smile," Becks interrupted.

Tyler frowned at Becks. "Why am I smiling when I'm discussing the potential demise of my mother's company?" he asked.

"Because you're the man who's going to save it for her and for the stockholders, Tyler," Becks said, with what Kelsey thought was just a hint of sarcasm.

Tyler seemed to notice it as well. "Becks, although you may disagree with my methods, I'm right about my mother's board," he said.

"Tyler, you don't need to prove it to me," Becks said. "You need to prove it to the shareholders. Start over."

Tyler squared his shoulders, smiled and began to speak.

"After the problems with the Koh Software integration…"

On Friday night, Tyler leaned back on the sofa and rested his head on Kelsey's shoulder. Kelsey stroked his hair gently. It was midnight, and they were sitting in her living room. After last night's lesson with Becks, she had made it known that Tyler needed to practice more if anyone was going to take him seriously. So they had left work, and come back to Kelsey's to practice.

"You're doing better," Kelsey said.

"I don't know how Lisa does this every day," Tyler said. "My jaws hurt from smiling."

"She's had a lot of practice," Kelsey pointed out.

"How am I going to be CEO?"

"Do you think that Lisa's still going to want you to be CEO after this?" Kelsey said.

"Of course. It's going to be my punishment for starting the proxy fight," Tyler replied.

"Seriously?"

"Kelsey, I've known Lisa my whole life. My starting the proxy fight is only going to make her pause long enough to deal with me for a month or two. By July, she'll be back on the road to world domination, and my being CEO is part of that plan."

Kelsey laughed. "World domination?" she asked.

"Wait until you get to know her," Tyler replied sincerely.

"Can't wait," Kelsey said doubtfully.

On Saturday morning, Kelsey met Jessica at Target. Tyler had stayed at Kelsey's until 2 a.m., and Kelsey had offered to let him sleep on the sofa, but Tyler had gone home, pointing out that there was no Jade to keep him out of Kelsey's bedroom.

"What do you think of this one?" Jessica asked, holding up a blue-and-green-striped baby onesie.

"So cute," Kelsey said. The onesie was soft and had a little brown bear on it.

"I'll get it," Jessica said.

"You should," Kelsey agreed.

"Will you be one of the babies' godparents?" Jessica asked.

"I'd be honored," Kelsey said in surprise. "But I'm not religious."

"It's fine. We haven't decided how to raise them anyway."

"You aren't going to raise them Catholic?"

Jessica shrugged. "Ryan hasn't even been baptized," she said. "He said it was up to me, and that he would even get baptized if I thought it was important, but I'm not sure. There's a lot of guilt that goes with being Catholic, and I'm not sure I want to raise my kids like that."

"Is there guilt with being Catholic, or guilt because of the way you were raised?" Kelsey asked.

"You have a point. I don't know, I have some time to think about it. But anyway, I want you to be a godparent."

"OK," Kelsey said happily.

Jessica shook a giraffe-shaped rattle. "Cute," she said, adding it to the red basket that Kelsey was carrying.

"How are you feeling?" Kelsey asked.

"Sick," Jessica said. "I'm eating so many ginger chews Bob might be better off buying the company."

"It won't last long though, right?" Kelsey asked in concern.

"I don't think so. Not much past the first trimester. It's OK, I'll just tough it out."

"Is Ryan cooking nice things for you?" Kelsey asked, knowing the answer.

Jessica smiled. "Ryan is doing everything for me. I didn't know he could be more attentive, but it's adorable."

"That's sweet," Kelsey said.

"And how is your renewed romance with Mr. Olsen?"

"Tyler's fine. Things are pretty much back to normal."

"And you haven't been caught by Ms. Olsen yet?"

"Not yet."

"Are you ready for when she finds out?" Jessica asked, putting another onesie into the basket.

Kelsey sighed. "Not really," she admitted.

"You'd better get ready," Jessica said seriously, brushing an auburn curl from her face.

"I know," Kelsey said. Tyler had discussed it with Kelsey as well. While Kelsey had been in Arizona, Tyler had restructured his trusts. With his birthday the previous September, two of Tyler's trusts had been released to his full control. He had taken them from the trustee and hired a new wealth manager to oversee them.

Tyler had suggested that Kelsey consider moving her assets from the office building in Port Townsend into a shell company, so they would be harder for Lisa to find, but since Lisa had given her the building, Kelsey wasn't confident that it would be worth the trouble. For the time being, the building would continue to be managed by her father and Papa Jefferson.

"Have you seen her lately?" Kelsey asked Jessica.

"Lisa? Thankfully, no. She's back in California. She told Ryan she's thrilled about being a grandmother though. Grannie Lisa."

Kelsey giggled at the name, and Jessica grinned. But then her face turned serious.

"In the meantime, the real grandmother still hasn't spoken to Ryan."

"She knows about the twins, though?"

"Bob called her," Jessica replied. "I just don't get Ryan."

"He still hasn't talked you about Cherie?"

"He just shuts down," Jessica shrugged. "I don't want to bring it up any more, because it just ruins our evening. But I think Bob is determined to bring Cherie out for the birth, so Ryan's going to have to get his act together."

"I hope he does," Kelsey said.

"Me too," Jessica said, picking up a pink teddy bear and setting it gently back down on the shelf. "Enough about Ryan. How are you? How's work?"

"Busy, thanks to my new client, Tyler."

"Tyler is your client?" Jessica asked.

"Bill assigned him to me."

"That's funny," Jessica said.

"So I've got to sit in on all of his meetings with his PR person, and do a bunch of research. Plus, Bill said I have to charge Tyler for every hour I spend talking about the proxy fight."

"Tyler won't care."

"I know. But it's weird."

"It's only a few more weeks. Then Lisa Olsen will have her explosion about your upcoming nuptials and Tyler's proxy fight."

"February 15," Kelsey sighed.

"The day World War Three begins," Jessica added.

On Sunday, Kelsey beamed when she saw Tyler waiting out on the sidewalk for her. He was holding a lone rose.

"And where am I supposed to put that?" Kelsey teased as she gave him a kiss. Tyler surveyed her. Kelsey was wearing running leggings and had her pink running jacket on.

Tyler grinned. "I have no idea. Someone was selling them next to the bus stop," he said, handing it to her.

"Thank you for thinking of me. I'll put it upstairs," she said, taking his hand and pulling him back inside her building.

A few minutes, and many kisses later, Tyler and Kelsey were running down First Avenue. It was the first time that they had exercised together in a long time, and Kelsey was so happy.

She turned to him, and her blonde ponytail whipped in the wind. "You're doing OK. You've been exercising without me," she said.

"Of course. I knew you'd make me start again when I asked you to marry me," Tyler replied.

"I want you to be healthy," Kelsey said.

"I know," Tyler said. "I've been working on it."

"I've noticed. I'm proud of you," Kelsey said, as they ran into Pioneer Square.

"Thanks," Tyler said.

"Thank you," Kelsey replied. "You've been working really hard for us."

"This wasn't fair to you," Tyler commented.

"No. It wasn't. But it wasn't your fault."

"I feel like it was," Tyler said.

"Your mother isn't your fault," Kelsey said wisely. "I certainly don't want to be held responsible for mine," she added.

Tyler grinned at her as they stopped for a light. She smiled at him. It was nice to see his chocolate-brown eyes sparkle again.

"Tyler, things are OK now," Kelsey said. "We know what to expect, and I'm not afraid."

"I'm glad," Tyler said, as they crossed the street.

They ran in silence for a moment, then Tyler said, "When this is over, what do you want?"

Kelsey looked at him, a bit puzzled. "What do you mean?"

"I mean that for the past three years, our relationship has been defined by my dramas. I want that to end, and I want us to build something for ourselves," Tyler replied.

"Are you planning on renouncing your inheritance? Disowning your parents?" Kelsey teased.

"I don't understand," Tyler admitted.

"Tyler, our lives together will always be defined by the situations that having two billion dollars brings into your life. It will also be at least partly defined by our crazy friends and relatives. That's OK. I know what I'm signing up for. I've had a preview."

"That doesn't bother you?" Tyler asked curiously.

Kelsey shook her head. "There's both good and bad. On both sides. We'll deal, because we have each other."

Tyler nodded as they ran past the stadiums. "I hate always reacting," he commented.

"Well, this time you won't be. You're starting the fight."

"I know," Tyler said thoughtfully.

"You don't have to," Kelsey said. "You haven't sent out the letter."

"I do have to," Tyler said definitively. "I don't have a choice."

Kelsey said nothing. She knew that for Tyler, this was his way of taking a stand.

"Either way, I support you," she finally said.

"Thank you," Tyler said. They ran in silence, until they reached Starbucks Center, their turnaround point. But as they headed back, just as they reached South Holgate, the skies opened, and the rain began to pour.

"Oh, no," Kelsey cried. But she wasn't unhappy. She was here with Tyler, and no amount of rain could dampen her spirits.

"We'll have to run faster," Tyler said.

Kelsey glanced at him. He seemed happy too. "Race you back," she said, brightly.

"You're on," Tyler said, and they dashed up the street.

As they entered downtown, Tyler detoured from First Avenue, up to Fourth.

"I'll make breakfast for you. You can change at my place and go home later," Tyler said.

"OK," Kelsey agreed as they ran on. Once they were in sight of Tyler's building, they sped up again. Kelsey grinned and raced Tyler to the front door.

"I win," she said.

Tyler laughed. "Let's get inside," he said, and they entered the building, breathless and soaked. The doorman smiled as they walked past him and went up to Tyler's apartment.

Tyler let them into the apartment, and said to Kelsey, "I'm going to go to the store and get some eggs."

"It's pouring!" Kelsey said.

"I'm drenched anyway. I'll be back in five," Tyler said, kissing her on the forehead. "Get dry," he said, as he left.

Kelsey took off her wet shoes and socks and left them by the table in the entry way. Barefoot, she made her way into Tyler's bathroom, closed the door and stripped out of her wet clothes. She wrapped a towel around herself and headed to Tyler's bedroom to find some dry clothes. She closed the door behind herself.

As she looked around, Kelsey heard the front door open.

That was quick, she thought to herself. She heard footsteps inside of the apartment.

Suddenly, the bedroom door opened.

Kelsey unconsciously wrapped the towel tighter, and Jeffrey walked in.

They looked at each other in surprise for a moment, then they heard keys in the front door.

Want my unreleased 5000-word story
Introducing the Billionaire Boys Club
and other free gifts from time to time?

Then join my mailing list at

http://www.caramillerbooks.com/inner-circle/

Subscribe now and read it now!

You can also follow me on Twitter and Facebook

Made in the USA
Middletown, DE
17 October 2023

40962958R00146